THE PRETZEL PAL

PRESENTS:

"THE TERRIBLE TWIST"

SEE ONE OF HORRORLAND'S SUPERVILLAINS CREATE BALLOON ANIMALS FROM VERY UNUSUAL MATERIALS

LIMITED-RUN SHOW WHILE GUESTS SUPPLIES LAST!

ALL AGES & ALL CREATURES SHOW.
TICKETS AVAILABLE AT THE CROCODILE CAFÉ,
GUILLOTINE MUSEUM, AND HAUNTED THEATRE.

HorrorLand

www.EnterHorrorLand.com

THE
PRETZEL PAL
PRESENTS:

"THE
TERRIBLE
TWIST"

SEE ONE
OF HORRORLAND'S
SUPER VILLAINS CREATE
BALLOON ANIMALS WITH
VERY UNUSUAL MATERIALS

LIMITED SHOW
SHOW WITH GUESTS
SUPPLIES LAST!

ESCAPE
HORRORLAND

ALL AGES & ALL CREATURES SHOW
TICKETS AVAILABLE AT THE CROCODILE CAFÉ
GUILLOTINE MUSEUM, AND HAUNTED THEATRE

www.EnterHorrorLand.com

GOOSEBUMPS HorrorLand™
ALL-NEW! ALL-TERRIFYING!

GOOSEBUMPS®
NOW WITH BONUS FEATURES!
LOOK IN THE BACK OF THE BOOK
FOR EXCLUSIVE AUTHOR INTERVIEWS AND MORE.

WELCOME TO CAMP SLITHER

R.L. STINE

SCHOLASTIC

Scholastic Children's Books
A division of Scholastic Ltd
Euston House, 24 Eversholt Street
London, NW1 1DB, UK
Registered office: Westfield Road, Southam, Warwickshire, CV47 0RA
SCHOLASTIC, GOOSEBUMPS, GOOSEBUMPS HORRORLAND, and
associated logos
are trademarks and/or registered trademarks of Scholastic Inc.

First published in the US in 2009 by Scholastic Inc.
This edition published in the UK by Scholastic Ltd, 2009
Goosebumps series created by Parachute Press, Inc.

ISBN 978 1407 10773 8
British Library Cataloguing-in-Publication Data.
A CIP catalogue record for this book is available from the British Library

Printed and bound by CPI Group (UK) Ltd, Croydon, CR0 4YY
Papers used by Scholastic Children's Books are made from wood grown in
sustainable forests.

12

www.scholastic.co.uk/zone

3 RIDES IN 1!

WELCOME TO CAMP SLITHER

1

You know that jumpy kind of feeling when you just can't keep still? You want to hop around or run really fast or do a crazy dance?

That's the feeling I had as I climbed on to the camp bus. Yeah, my sister Heather and I were totally *psyched*.

We love summer camp. We love being outdoors and hanging out with other kids – and *no parents* around. Heather and I are really into animals and learning about bugs and snakes and all kinds of creatures.

We have two rabbits we keep in a pen behind our garage. And we have a hamster and an old box turtle and two dogs – Rusty and Max – one for each of us, although they both like Heather better than me.

Camp Hither is supposed to be an excellent wilderness camp. At least, that's what Mom and Dad said. So yes, Heather and I were excited.

3

My little sister – I'm twelve and she's ten – had only one complaint. "I'm always away from home for my birthday," she said. "So I can never have a birthday party."

"So?" I said. "Who told you to be born in the summer?"

She gave me that cold stare she always gives me, with her eyes half closed and her mouth all twisted. "Boone, give me a ding-dong break."

That's one of her favourite expressions. She heard it from our grandmother. Mom and Dad think she's a riot. I don't really get it. Who *talks* like that who isn't, like, eighty years old?

Heather doesn't look like she's in the same family as me. I'm tall and thin. I have short, straight black hair and dark brown eyes.

I'm a jumpy kind of dude. I mean, I've got a lot of energy. It's hard to sit still. I'm always tapping my fingers on something or bopping around.

Dad says I'm the original Energizer Bunny. Ha-ha. Why does everyone in my family think they're a comedian?

Heather has very curly hair and green eyes. She's about a foot shorter than me, and a little chubby. I'd never tell her that. I mean, I learned my lesson.

Once I was kind of angry, and I called her Chubs. I know. It was dumb.

She gave me a really hard punch in the stomach.

Which I still think about. I walked around bent over, looking like the number seven, for about a week.

Heather likes to punch people. She thinks she's so cute, she can get away with it.

She's very strange. She likes to wear all kinds of bracelets and rings and sparkly things and dangly plastic earrings.

I told her no one else in her class wears that stuff. And she stuck her tongue out at me and made a loud spitting noise.

Anyway, we heaved our bags into the luggage compartment of the yellow camp bus. Then we said goodbye to Mom and Dad, with hugs all around.

Heather gave me a push towards the bus door. I told you, she's always pushing and punching me. She's totally dangerous.

I climbed the three steps on to the bus. It took a while for my eyes to adjust. I could see a lot of kids were already on board.

Heather followed me as I started down the narrow aisle to the back. And I heard the bus driver mutter, "Two more victims." Then he shut the door.

What did he mean by that?

I saw two empty seats on the aisle near the back of the bus. I plopped down into one of them and shoved my backpack under the seat in front of me.

Some kids near the driver were tossing a blue football back and forth. Two girls were singing a camp song I knew from my old camp.

The bus made a roaring sound – and lurched forward before Heather sat down. She fell on me, and her elbow jammed right into my gut.

"Oof."

Did that hurt? Three guesses, and they're all *yes*.

My sister didn't apologize, of course. Instead, she pulled herself up and yelled at the bus driver, "Give me a ding-dong break!"

That made some kids laugh. Heather didn't care. She sat down and started talking instantly to the girl next to her.

I turned to look at the kid next to me. He was staring through big black-framed glasses at a manga book in his lap. He was moving his lips as he read it. He didn't look up.

Why didn't he say hi or something? I guessed maybe he was shy.

He was about my age. He had white-blond hair cut really short and pale blue eyes behind the glasses. He was maybe the palest guy I ever saw.

You know what flashed into my mind? A zombie in a movie I watched over at my friend's house a couple of nights before.

The dude wasn't a freak or anything. It's just that, with that white-blond hair, everything blended into everything.

And he was wearing a white T-shirt and baggy white shorts.

And what was he squeezing in the hand that didn't hold the manga book? Was that a rabbit's foot?

"Where's the rest of the rabbit?" I asked. "In your backpack?"

I know it was a lame joke. But I thought it was a *little* funny. He smiled. But he didn't laugh. He *did* raise his eyes from the comic, though.

He held up the rabbit's foot. "It's kind of a good-luck thing," he said.

I took it from his hand. Yucko. It was wet from his sweat.

"I'm Boone Dixon," I said. "That's my sister, Heather." I pointed.

"I'm Ronny McDonald," I thought he said. A car horn honked. I couldn't really hear him.

I laughed. "Your name is Ronald McDonald? Weird!"

He shook his head. "*Roddy* McDonald."

I handed him back his rabbit's foot. "You really think you're gonna need good luck?" I asked.

He shrugged his narrow shoulders. "I heard some things about this camp," he said softly. "Kinda scary things."

"Like what?" I asked.

He shrugged again. He glanced out the window. I don't think he wanted to talk about it. "Snakes," he said finally.

I waited for him to say more. Farms and flat green fields passed by outside the bus window.

"Some kids at school said stuff about snakes in the lake," Roddy said, turning to me. Behind his glasses, his eyes were wide. The kid really looked frightened.

"These kids read about it online. They said the counsellors make you swim with the snakes," Roddy said. He twirled his damp rabbit's foot in his hand. "You have to swim across the lake. And the snakes . . . the snakes. . ."

I felt sorry for the dude. Some kids at his school

8

told him a bunch of baloney, and he believed it.

"I tried to tell my parents," Roddy said. "But they thought I was making it up so I wouldn't have to go to camp."

"You're a first-timer, right?" I said. "Don't you know kids always tell scary camp stories to frighten new campers? It's just what kids do. You know. It's a tradition."

"Not this time," Roddy said. "They didn't make it up."

The manga book fell out of his lap. He leaned down to get it. When he sat back up, his face was still filled with fear.

"Know what they call this camp?" he asked.

"Sure," I said. "Camp Hither."

"No," he said, shaking his head. "Everyone who goes there calls it Camp *Slither*. Because of all the snakes."

I laughed. He looked so serious, I just couldn't help it. "Roddy," I said, "I've been to two different wilderness camps. Camps are fun. I had an awesome time. So will you."

He swallowed hard. "Those kids told me other snake stories—"

"They made them up!" I cried. "They were just trying to scare you."

He stared at me.

"Tell you what," I said. "Let's ask some kids who were at Camp Hither last summer. They'll tell you the truth."

I stood up. The bus was filled with campers. Every seat. Kids were laughing and talking.

I cupped my hands around my mouth and shouted, "Hey, everyone! Everyone! Who was at this camp last year? I need to talk to you."

Some kids turned around to stare at me. No hands went up.

"How many?" I asked. "Don't all raise your hands at once."

No one. Not one.

I gazed down the long aisle. "All new campers?" I asked.

Some kids nodded their heads. Others turned around and went back to what they were doing.

I dropped back on to my seat. "Weird," I muttered.

"See? I'm right, Boone," Roddy said. "No one ever goes back to this camp."

His whole body shuddered. "M-maybe it's because no one survives," he stammered.

"Roddy – that's impossible," I said. "This is the bus for new kids, that's all. They probably sent another bus for old campers. There will be lots of—"

I stopped short – and gasped. I heard a sharp rattling sound. Right next to me.

"A snake!" Roddy screamed. "It's a SNAKE!"

3

"NOOOOOOOOO!"

Kids screamed. Two girls cracked heads as they tried to dive out of their seats. Roddy raised his arms in front of him like a shield.

I heard the rattle again. The warning from a rattlesnake that it's about to strike.

I turned – and saw Heather laughing. She had her hand raised. She was shaking the bracelet around her wrist. Making it rattle.

Dad brought the bracelet back from a business trip to India. It's a silver bangle with pebbles inside. The pebbles make a loud rattle when she shakes her arm.

I should have known!

That rattling bracelet fools me every time. I'm sure that's why Heather wears it.

I grabbed Heather's hand and pushed it down to her lap.

She shrugged. "Oops. Didn't mean to cause a

ding-dong *riot*!"

"False alarm!" I shouted. "False alarm! There's no snake!"

Kids climbed back into their seats. It took a long time for everyone to calm down.

I turned to Roddy. He was pressed against the window. He squeezed his rabbit's foot. He looked even paler than before.

"See what I mean?" he said. "Everyone's freaked out. Know why? Because they've heard the stories about Camp Hither, too."

"Roddy, there aren't any snakes in the lake," I repeated. "The kids who told you that were just trying to scare you."

"They told me other stories," he said softly, gazing out the window. "About a snake. A very big snake."

I shook my head. I started to tell him to lighten up. But my sister tapped me on the shoulder.

"Do you think Mom and Dad will send my birthday presents to camp?" she asked. "Or do you think they'll forget like last summer?"

I shook my fist in the air. "Heather, do you want to live to be eleven? Then, *stop talking about your birthday*!"

"Shut your dirty doodad!" she snapped.

That's another one of our grandmother's favourite expressions. I don't know why Heather keeps repeating them. Is she weird or what?

A few minutes later, the bus pulled off the road and began to bounce along a gravel driveway. We passed a large wooden sign that read: WELCOME TO CAMP HITHER! LIFE IN THE WILD!

"Hey, we're here!" I cried.

Kids cheered and shouted, bounced up and down in their seats, and slapped high fives. The bus driver honked the horn five or six times.

We rolled through thick woods. Patches of purple and red wild flowers lined the gravel drive. Through the trees, I could see a blue lake in the distance, surrounded by tall grass.

The bus squealed to a stop. Everyone jumped up. We pushed and shoved each other in our rush to get out of the bus.

Blinking in the bright sunlight, I gazed around. The bus had parked in front of a group of small cabins used for supplies. They were made of wood, painted white.

I saw swingball poles in front of each cabin. And at one end, a wide, grassy football field. Behind the field, a steep green hill led to more buildings. Thick woods surrounded the whole camp.

The bus driver started to pull our bags from the luggage hold. And a grinning man came running towards us across the gravel car park.

He was tall and thin and very tanned. He had a black moustache and sleek, shiny black hair brushed straight back from his forehead.

"Yo, everyone! Yo!" he called, waving as he came trotting towards us. "Welcome!"

He wore baggy khaki shorts and a brown sweatshirt with a large coiled snake printed on the front. The snake had its jaws open as if it was ready to snap.

Roddy poked me in the ribs. "See what I mean?" he whispered. "See? It's all about snakes."

"Roddy, it's a *wilderness* camp – remember?" I said. "Forget those stories. Forget—"

The man turned around and I read the name on the back of his sweatshirt. In snaky black letters, it said:

DR CRAWLER.

14

4

Roddy's eyes bulged. He poked me again.

I jumped away from him. The kid was giving me *bruises*.

"It's just the dude's name," I told him. "Stop being so crazy."

Roddy lowered his eyes. "S-sorry," he muttered. "I'll try. I . . . I don't know why my parents sent me to this camp. I said I'd rather go to *diet* camp! Anything but this!"

I laughed. I thought he was making a joke. But he was totally serious.

"Welcome, people!" Dr Crawler shouted. "Welcome! I'm the head counsellor here."

He had a soft voice. When he spoke, his black moustache wiggled up and down.

He brushed a fly off my shoulder. "What's your name, son?" he asked.

"Boone Dixon," I said.

He smiled. "Welcome to Camp Hither." He

waved to a tall black-haired boy in long blue basketball shorts and a sleeveless blue net T-shirt with a Nike swoosh across the front. The boy was helping to unload the bus.

"Nathan, over here!" Dr Crawler shouted. "Boone is one of your campers."

Nathan came trotting over. He was maybe eighteen or nineteen. His black hair was scraggly and fell down to his shoulders. He had a silver ring in one ear.

He had a fake tattoo of a bat on the back of one hand. He wiped sweat off his forehead with the front of his T-shirt.

"Whussup?" he asked. "How ya doin'? Guess I'm your counsellor."

Dr Crawler rounded up the other kids in our group. Roddy was one. And two other guys our age, Sid and Kelly.

They were both tall, with short brown hair and brown eyes. Kelly had a nice smile. Sid looked kind of serious.

Nathan lined the four of us up in front of him. "You're my guys," he said. "You got a problem, you come to me."

"I've got a problem," Roddy murmured.

Nathan squinted at him. "What's wrong?"

"Are there a lot of snakes in the lake?" Roddy asked.

Nathan shrugged. "I don't think so. Why? You

like snakes? I could find you some snakes. You guys want to go on a snake hunt?"

"No!" Roddy shouted. "I mean, I *don't* like snakes."

Nathan's eyes flashed. He grinned at Roddy. "Ever eat snake meat? Yummmm."

Roddy made a disgusted face. "That's *sick*."

"What does it taste like?" Kelly asked.

"Kinda like chicken," Nathan said. "Only snakier." He waved one arm. "Follow me, guys."

He led us away from the car park, towards the wooden cabins up ahead. Our trainers thudded on the soft earth.

"Where are we going?" Roddy asked. "To our cabin? Does our cabin have a bathroom in it?"

"You have to see the nurse first," Nathan replied.

"The nurse?" Roddy squeaked. "Are we getting a shot?"

"Take a deep breath," Nathan told him. "You're kinda wired, aren't you?"

"But I don't get it," Roddy said, trotting to keep up with the rest of us. "Why do we have to see the nurse?"

"It's the rule," Nathan said.

The nurse greeted us in the doorway of her little shack. She looked about as old as my grandmother. She had a red-and-white baseball cap pulled down over her grey hair. She wore a plaid flannel shirt over baggy jeans.

"Y'all can call me Nurse April," she said. "I'm always here. If y'all can't find me in my clinic, look for me at the mess hall."

Nurse April raised a tall spray can in one hand. "This won't hurt a bit," she said.

She grabbed my shoulder with the other hand. And began spraying a sticky orange liquid on my skin.

My skin tingled. I suddenly felt weird. "Hey!" I shouted. "What are you *doing*? Stop! What *is* this stuff?"

"It's superglue," Nathan said. "I like my guys to stick together." He laughed.

"Y'all will get used to Nathan," Nurse April said. "He has a strange sense of humour ... because he comes from another planet."

She turned me around and sprayed the back of my neck. "Relax, fella," she said. "It's called Sun-Glo. It's sun protection."

She moved to Sid and started spraying it up and down one of his legs. The orange liquid dripped down on to his white sports socks.

"We are very careful about sun protection here at Camp Hither," Nurse April said.

"You'll find cans of Sun-Glo in your cabin," Nathan said. "I want you guys to spray yourselves with it twice a day."

Nurse April finished spraying Sid and started on Roddy's arms. "We want to keep you safe," she said.

My skin felt a little itchy. Sid and Kelly waved their arms in the air, trying to get the sunscreen lotion to dry.

Other campers were lined up outside, waiting for their turns. When we were all covered in the stuff, Nathan led us to our cabin.

The cabins were spread out along a trail through tall, shady trees. As we walked, I could see the football field, and in the distance, the lake, shimmering in the sunlight.

The girls' cabins came first. The boys' cabins were deeper in the woods.

The cabins all had name signs above their doors. We passed Cobra, Rattler and then Black Mamba.

Nathan stopped outside a small cabin with peeling paint and one boarded-up window. The cabin was named Cottonmouth.

"Maybe you noticed," he said. "The cabins here are all named after poisonous snakes."

"That's awesome," I said. Sid and Kelly agreed.

Of course, Roddy made a face. "It's creepy," he muttered.

We followed Nathan into Cottonmouth. It was just big enough for two bunk beds and two dressers. A poster of a big brown iguana hung between the two bunk beds. Two bulbs hanging on cords from the ceiling were the only lights.

"Can I have a bottom bunk?" Roddy asked. "I toss and turn a lot in my sleep."

"No problem," I said. "I'll take the top."

A couple of junior counsellors walked up to our cabin with our bags piled on a cart. Nathan told us to grab our bags and put our stuff away.

Roddy tugged at Nathan's shirt. "Did you know kids call this place Camp *Slither*?" he asked.

Nathan laughed. "No. Never heard that one. Pretty good."

Roddy didn't give up. "Well, did you hear any stories about a giant snake that lives in the lake?"

Nathan laughed again. "Do you believe everything you hear?"

"No," Roddy started. "But—"

"Forget all those scary stories," Nathan told him. "We're here to have fun, right? And to learn about the outdoors?"

Sid and Kelly were staring at Roddy. Like he was some kind of weirdo.

I felt sorry for the kid. He was so frightened. I hoped he wasn't going to be a pain all summer.

"Hurry. Unpack," Nathan said. "Then shove your bags under the bunks. First camp meeting is in half an hour. I'll come back to take you to it."

He ran off. The screen door slammed

behind him.

We started to pull stuff out of our bags. I turned to Kelly and Sid. "You guys been here before?"

They shook their heads. We were all first-timers.

Roddy held up his toothbrush and deodorant. "Where's the bathroom?"

"Didn't you see it?" Kelly said. "We passed it on the trail. It's that long building that isn't painted."

Roddy let out a sigh. He pulled a flashlight from his bag and placed it on the floor next to the bed.

Kelly picked up a can of Sun-Glo and squirted Sid on the back of the neck. Sid shrieked and dropped the stack of T-shirts he was holding. "Hey – what's the big idea?"

Kelly laughed. "Sun protection!" he said.

Sid pulled the spray can from Kelly's hand and let Kelly have it on the front of his shirt. I grabbed another can off the windowsill and sprayed Sid on the back of the neck, too.

We had an excellent spray battle. Even Roddy got into the act. A few seconds later, all four of us were laughing our heads off and dripping with the orange glop.

"Better get changed," I said. "It's almost time for the camp meeting."

I started to pull my wet, sticky shirt off – but stopped.

I suddenly felt strange again. My skin tingled like before, but worse. It felt all prickly.

I gazed at my hands – and gasped. My skin was scaly. It had all these little cracks and lines all over it.

Weird. I scratched the back of my hand. And a long strip of skin peeled off in my fingers!

I glanced over at the other guys. They seemed to be fine. No scratching. No tingling. No peeling skin.

It's probably just dry skin, I told myself. I decided to ignore it.

Nathan led us to the Meeting Ground. It was in a round clearing in the woods on the far side of the football field.

Kids laughed and talked as we crossed the field. Some guys were singing a funny rap song. Heather came running up to me. Her curly hair bounced as she ran.

"How's it going? What cabin are you in?" I asked her.

"Three guesses." She rattled her bracelet.

"You're in Rattler?"

She laughed. "Boone, you're a genius."

Sid and Kelly picked up long twigs. They started slapping them against each other in a wild sword fight as we walked. Those guys never quit.

Roddy walked between Heather and me. Kids tossed a red frisbee back and forth. "Look out!" someone shouted. It bounced off Roddy's back.

He let out a cry.

He probably thinks he was attacked by a snake! I thought.

But Roddy got it together quickly. He picked up the frisbee and sent it sailing back to the kids. A nice toss.

"Roddy wants to tell us another horror story about a giant snake that lives in the lake," I told Heather.

"It's not a horror story," Roddy protested. "It's a legend about Hither Lake. A kid told me it was true."

Heather rattled her bracelet in Roddy's face. "Go, Rattlers! Rattlers rule!" she cried. She did a freaky snake dance around Roddy and me.

My sister is totally disturbing.

"What's the legend?" I asked Roddy.

"This guy told me about a GIANT diamondback water snake," Roddy said. "The snake is *giganto*. Really. It's as big as TWO alligators."

"Whoa," I said. "That's a *big* snake. And it lives in the lake?"

Roddy nodded. "Its name is *Serpo*. And it

needs to be fed. If it isn't fed, it crawls out of the lake – and attacks the camp."

"That's doo-dah nasty," Heather said.

We were nearing the Meeting Ground. Kids were sitting in a semicircle near a low white stone wall.

"How do they feed Serpo?" I asked Roddy.

He swallowed. "I know you're not going to believe this, Boone. But this is what the kids at school told me."

"Tell," Heather said.

"Once during the summer, the counsellors make all the campers swim across Lake Hither. And Serpo pulls some kids down. For *food*. That's how they feed him. And when he's finished eating the campers, their bare bones wash up on shore."

Roddy looked so serious, Heather and I burst out laughing.

"That's not true. That's from a movie!" Heather said. "Bye!" She ran off across the grass to join some other girls from her cabin.

"I *said* you wouldn't believe me," Roddy muttered.

We followed Nathan to the Meeting Ground. The four of us sat down in the grass.

The low wall curved behind us. We faced a tall black rock, almost diamond-shaped. Behind it, we could see a steep grassy hill with a building at the top.

Thick woods surrounded us. Behind the trees,

the afternoon sun was starting to drop.

Dr Crawler came out and stood in front of the rock. He had changed into jeans, sandals and a green-and-blue sweatshirt that said CAMP HITHER across the front.

"This is our welcome meeting," he announced. "And so, let me say . . . welcome! Here at Camp Hither, we want you to have the most fun you can in the great outdoors."

Someone popped a loud bubblegum bubble. Kids burst out laughing.

Dr Crawler's moustache curled up as he smiled. "I see a lot of you are *already* having fun!" he said. "Well, things are always *popping* here at Camp Hither!"

It was a lame joke. But a few kids laughed at it.

Dr Crawler slapped his hand on the black rock. "Let me tell you the story of the Meeting Rock," he said. "We have many stories to tell here at Camp Hither, and this rock. . ."

I couldn't hear the rest of what he was saying. His voice was suddenly drowned out by a loud hissing sound.

The sound rose like a siren . . . loud . . . shrill. . .

It seemed to float down from the hill.

Roddy pressed his hands over his ears. His eyes grew wide with fright. "I told you," he whispered. "Snakes. Snakes *everywhere*!"

27

Dr Crawler kept talking. Didn't he hear it? Was he just ignoring it?

Roddy jumped to his feet. "What is that sound?" he cried.

Dr Crawler's smile faded. He squinted at Roddy. "Wow, you must never leave your house," he said. "Haven't you ever heard crickets before?"

Everyone was staring at Roddy.

"It doesn't sound like crickets," a girl said. She had to shout over the loud hissing noises.

"I promise you city kids, that's what crickets sound like," Dr Crawler said. "Tell you what. Tomorrow, we'll all go on a long hike. It'll be a cricket hunt."

Roddy sat back down next to me. The hissing sound died suddenly. It just cut out, like someone turning off a radio.

I turned to Roddy and whispered, "It *could*

28

have been crickets," I said. "Just ignore it."

But the sound got me thinking. Was the hill really crawling with snakes? Was Dr Crawler trying to keep it from us? Maybe he just didn't want us to get scared on our first day of camp.

Dr Crawler started talking about camp activities. I kept thinking about Roddy and how scared he was. And I kept waiting for the hissing sound to start up again.

"Our Cabin Wars begin next week," Dr Crawler said. He kept slapping the weird-shaped rock as he talked. "It's cabin versus cabin. I'll explain the point system later. But believe me, people – Cabin Wars get pretty intense. I mean, it's take-no-prisoners around here!"

"Cottonmouth rules!" Kelly shouted.

Dr Crawler laughed.

Kids started shouting out the names of their cabins.

"I *told* you it gets intense!" Dr Crawler exclaimed. "And, of course, the big event – the *biggest* competition – is the swimming race across Lake Hither."

I saw Roddy shiver. And I knew he was thinking about Serpo, the enormous snake at the bottom of the lake.

When the meeting broke up, I ran over to Nathan. He and two other counsellors were pulling chocolate bars out of a backpack and passing them to each other.

Nathan turned when he saw me. "Sorry. You're too late. None left," he said. The other two counsellors wandered off, chewing loudly.

"I don't want a chocolate bar," I said. "I have a question. Tell me the truth about the hissing."

Nathan shrugged. "Yeah, I heard it, too," he said. "I think it was just the wind or something. Catch you later."

He called to the other counsellors and went running after them.

The *wind*? Was Nathan totally clueless? Or was he hiding the truth from me?

That night, just as I was getting used to the lumpy, hard mattress . . . just as my eyes were closing . . . the hissing started up again.

Next morning, Roddy woke me up with a shrill wail of horror. "SNAKE!" he screamed. "Ohhh, help me! SNAKE!"

I jerked straight up in my top bunk – and smacked my head on the ceiling. Pain shot down my body.

I dropped to the floor and glanced all around. I didn't see a snake anywhere.

"SNAKE! SNAKE!" Roddy screeched.

Was he having a bad dream? I grabbed his shoulders and shook him. Kelly and Sid hurried up beside me.

"Where?" I demanded. "Where is the snake?"

"It's . . . it's inside MY HEAD!" Roddy cried.

Roddy's whole body shuddered and shook. He pointed frantically to his ear. "It's INSIDE me!"

I grabbed his head and tilted it to get a better look inside his ear.

And saw something green wiggling around in there.

8

Carefully, I lowered my thumb and forefinger to Roddy's ear – and pinched them around the wriggling green thing. Gently, I tugged it out.

"Oh, gross!" Sid cried.

Kelly let out a low moan.

I stared at the fuzzy caterpillar between my fingers. "How did this get in your ear?"

Roddy was still shaking. Tears rolled down his face. "It . . . it must have crawled in while I was asleep. I . . . thought it was a snake."

"Just a caterpillar," I said. I tossed it out the cabin window.

"Sick," Kelly said, scratching his ears. "That was way sick."

"I don't want to think about it ever again," Sid said.

"Ooh, my ear still itches," Roddy moaned. "Hey, Boone – what if it laid eggs in there? What if, in a few weeks, a million caterpillars hatch inside my head?"

"I don't think caterpillars lay eggs," I said.

A few minutes later, Nathan came to make sure we were awake. He was surprised to find us already getting dressed. He made us spray ourselves with Sun-Glo before we could go to breakfast.

We had egg sandwiches on English muffins in the mess hall. Not too shabby.

I saw Heather at a table across the long room. I walked over to her. "Did you sleep?" I asked her.

"Diggety diggety," she said.

The other girls at the table laughed.

"Did you hear the hissing?" I asked.

"Diggety diggety," Heather repeated.

"Did you hear there's a three-kilometre hike this morning?"

"Diggety diggety."

I could see I wasn't going to get anywhere with her. She does this to me all the time. She thinks she's a riot.

"Diggety diggety to you, too," I muttered. I went back to my table and had another egg sandwich.

Dr Crawler had promised us we'd hike, and that's what we did. The counsellors led the whole camp along a dirt trail that twisted through the trees.

It was pretty awesome. I walked with Nathan, Sid and Kelly. I made sure I kept ahead of Roddy. I wanted to enjoy the forest. I didn't want to hear or think about snakes or caterpillars crawling into anyone's ears.

We didn't see a single snake. We saw some amazing birds. Two bright red cardinals perched on a low tree limb right above our heads. They stared down at us as if daring us to come closer.

We saw a lot of chipmunks, some fast-running field mice, and brown rabbits. The rabbits froze on two legs and stood as still as statues, waiting for us to pass.

Sid kept snapping pictures with his mobile phone. He stopped suddenly when we saw a family of skunks cross the path up ahead.

We all stopped. There were five skunks walking in a single line. The mother walked in front, and four little ones followed.

"Keep downwind," Nathan whispered, waving us back. "Keep downwind."

I guess he meant, "don't let the skunks smell you". I froze like everyone else. No one moved or talked till the skunk family was long out of sight.

Then we all started talking and laughing at once. And everyone kept repeating, "Keep downwind, keep downwind." It was the joke of the morning.

By the time we got back to camp, the sun was high in the sky. And beating down on us. I was hot and sweaty, almost as smelly as a skunk.

Nathan gathered Sid, Kelly, Roddy and me outside our cabin. "Swimming trunks," he said. "Get moving, guys. Swimming trunks. We need a nice swim in the lake."

I saw the flash of fear in Roddy's eyes. But I didn't care. A cool swim in the lake was just what I needed.

"Swimming trunks!" Nathan ordered.

"And keep downwind," I added.

A few minutes later, the four of us were standing on the shore of Lake Hither. Tall grass ended a few metres from the water, leaving a muddy beach.

The lake was shaped like a perfect circle. The water shimmered so brightly in the sunlight, I could barely see the land on the other side.

A short dock made of wood planks stretched out into the lake. The dock had two rowing boats and a sailing boat tethered to it. They bobbed against each other in the gently lapping water.

Two tall stacks of black inner tubes were piled at one side of the dock. I took a step into the water. Warmer than I expected. The cool mud oozed between my toes.

I took another step – and a hand grabbed my shoulder, pulling me back. "Boone – check it out."

It was Roddy. He pointed to a deep rut in the muddy shore. "I'll bet the giant snake Serpo made that track," he said. "Look. He came out of the water. Recently."

I rolled my eyes. "Roddy, Nathan wouldn't let us swim here if there was a giant snake."

Roddy kept staring at the rut in the mud and shaking his head.

Nathan stepped beside us. He hitched up his long grey swimming trunks. He pushed his stringy hair out of his eyes and gazed at Roddy. "I'm worried about you, dude," he said.

Roddy blinked. "Huh? Me?"

"I heard what you said," Nathan replied. "About the giant snake and everything." He kicked at the rut until he filled it with mud.

"I'm gonna prove to you how safe this lake is," Nathan told Roddy. "I'm going in first. Watch."

Nathan spun around. He took off, running past us. His feet kicked up mud and then splashed water as he ran.

He stretched his arms in front of him and did a surface dive into the lake. We could see him swimming underwater smoothly, going deeper, then rising back up.

He surfaced, maybe four or five metres from

us. Not far from the shore. He motioned for us to join him. "Water's fine!" he called.

Then suddenly there was a big splash. Nathan's arms shot straight up in the air. He opened his mouth in a terrifying, shrill cry.

"Ohhh . . . *help*! It's GOT me!"

Water flew up all around him – and Nathan shot straight down. His chest slid under. Then his head. . .

His hands moved over the surface for a second, as if trying to grab on. Then they disappeared, pulled down under the tossing water.

The four of us stood frozen on the muddy shore, not moving, not breathing.

Waiting. . .

But Nathan didn't come back up.

"Serpo!" Roddy shrieked, jumping up and down, waving his arms like a wild man. "Serpo! I *told* you! It KILLED him!"

I stared at the dark green water. So still, lapping softly against the muddy shore.

A chill rolled down my back. Something had definitely pulled Nathan down. And he wasn't coming up.

"I'll find him!" I shouted to the others.

I took a running start – and leaped into the water. The cold shocked my body. But I ran till the water was over my knees. Then I did a surface dive and plunged underwater.

I opened my eyes. Pulled myself along the shallow bottom.

The water was green and clear. *Nathan – where are you? Where?*

No sign of him. I could feel panic tighten my chest.

And then my heart stopped as something wrapped around my ankle.

Scrpo!

I struggled to the surface, gasping and choking. I tried to kick free, but I was being pulled back down. I twisted around to try to see what had me in its grip.

Nathan! He let go of my ankle. Then he rose up and slapped the water with both hands. He spat a gusher of water at me.

"Hey – I'm only joking with you!" he shouted. "Counsellors have to have some fun, too!" He splashed around, laughing his head off.

My heart was pounding like thunder. What a mean joke!

Kelly and Sid came running into the water. The three of us grabbed Nathan and dunked him under.

We had a good time wrestling around, splashing each other, just goofing. The water felt awesome. I spun away and began swimming out into deeper water.

When I turned back, I saw Roddy still close to the shore. He was only in up to his knees. And even from out in the water, I could see the worried look on his face.

Poor guy, I thought. *He's not going to have any fun here.*

"Think I'll go back to the cabin!" Roddy called to us. I watched him walk away from the shore, his head down.

I had no idea that was the last time I'd ever see him here.

10

One hour later, Sid, Kelly and I were on our bunks in the cabin, just hanging out. Sid sat on the edge of his bed, playing a racing game on his PSP. His thumbs were going wild, and crashing sounds blared from the little speaker.

Above him, Kelly was taking a nap in the top bunk. One arm dangled down and kept bumping Sid's head. But Sid was too into his game to brush it away.

I was writing a note to Mom and Dad. I told them Heather and I gave the camp a big thumbs-up – so far.

Then the cabin door swung open, and Nathan burst in, followed by two other counsellors.

Sid didn't look up from his game. Kelly rolled over, still asleep.

The three counsellors had serious looks on their faces. They crossed the room to Roddy's bed, under mine. Nathan bent down and slid

Roddy's bag out from under the bunk.

"What's up?" I asked.

"We're packing up Roddy's stuff," Nathan replied.

"Which is his drawer?" a counsellor named Leo asked.

I pointed. "You're packing him up?" I asked. "Where's he going?"

"Home," Nathan said.

That made Sid look up. "He's leaving?" he asked.

Nathan nodded. He and Leo and the other guy began shoving clothes and other gear into the bag. "He didn't like it here," Nathan said.

"It happens sometimes," Leo muttered.

"He decided to go home," Nathan told me. "He said to say goodbye to you guys."

"But . . . but . . . we just saw him!" I stammered.

"It was kind of a sudden thing," Leo said. He jammed Roddy's flip-flops into the bag. "Where's his toothbrush and stuff?"

"Where is Roddy now?" Sid asked. "Maybe the three of us could go say goodbye to him."

"Too late," Nathan said. "He already left. On the bus."

"We're sending his stuff home after him," the other counsellor said.

Leo shrugged. "The dude just didn't like it here."

Nathan zipped the bag shut. He picked it up and turned to leave. The three counsellors tromped out the door. The screen door slammed behind them.

Kelly jerked straight up, wide-awake. "Hey, what's up?"

"Roddy took a hike," Sid told him. "He went home."

Kelly blinked. "On the *second day* of camp?"

"Yeah. It's weird," Sid said.

"Too weird," I said. "I don't think I believe those counsellors."

Sid shrugged. "Why would they lie?"

"Why would Roddy leave so soon?" I said. "Sure, he was frightened. But I don't think he was frightened enough to go home after one day."

Outside the open cabin window, the loud hissing started again. It started suddenly, as if someone had flipped a switch.

No way it could be crickets, I decided. *Too loud and too shrill. And why would all the crickets be up at the top of the hill?*

"Too many mysteries here," I muttered.

I jumped down from the top bunk. "Look. That manga book Roddy was reading." I picked it up from his bed. "Wouldn't he take it with him for the ride home?"

"And why didn't he come back and pack up his own stuff?" Kelly asked.

The hissing sound rose, growing more and more shrill, like steam shooting out of a hundred tea kettles.

"Listen, guys," I said. "I don't know about you, but I hate mysteries. So, I've been thinking. . ."

They leaned closer to hear me over the hissing.

"Here's my plan. . . " I said.

11

"We wait till everyone is asleep. An hour or so after lights out," I said. "We sneak out of here. We climb the hill. And we find out what's making that hissing sound. OK? Are you with me?"

They both shook their heads.

"No way," Sid said. "I don't want to get in trouble the first week. I like it here. I don't want to be sent home."

"I'm not going up there in the dark," Kelly said. "No way. Not on a bet."

"How about if I *dare* you?" I asked.

Sid went back to his game. "No way," he repeated.

Kelly picked up Roddy's manga book and took it up to his bunk to read.

OK. So they were both too chicken. But I knew one person who would sneak up the hill with me. One other person who hates mysteries as much as I do...

*　　*　　*

That night, I didn't get undressed. I climbed under the blanket with all my clothes on.

I tucked a flashlight beside me. I didn't want to forget it.

Sid and Kelly fell asleep quickly. I listened to the hissing sound outside the window. And I kept checking the time on my watch.

I guess I fell asleep for an hour or so. When I checked my watch again, it was a few minutes before midnight. Time for action.

I grabbed the flashlight and slid down silently to the floor. I crept out of the cabin and closed the screen door gently behind me.

It was a cool, breezy night. I saw a pale half-moon hanging low in the sky. The hissing sound rose and fell. Over and over.

I crept away from the row of cabins. Then I turned and started walking over the tall grass to the hill.

I was wearing flip-flops, and I could feel the cold, wet dew on my feet. A gust of wind made me shiver. I wished I had worn a sweatshirt and jeans instead of a flimsy T-shirt and shorts.

Something scampered across my feet. Probably a chipmunk or a field mouse. I clicked on the flashlight. Too late to see what it was.

I held the light down close to the grass. It made a tiny circle in front of me. I hoped no one was awake to see it.

The grass grew taller at the foot of the hill. Cold, wet blades brushed my knees. Grass curled around my ankles like snakes.

I gasped when I heard a sharp rattling sound. Close by.

I jumped back.

It took me a few seconds to remember it was Heather's bracelet. She jumped out of the darkness. "Boo!"

"Not funny," I whispered. "And you didn't scare me."

"Maybe a little?" she asked.

I shook my head. "No way."

"Diggety doughnut," she said. She pointed her flashlight beam up the steep hill. "Are we really going up there?"

"You volunteered," I said, shivering. "You said you were as brave as me."

"Braver," she said. She poked me in the ribs with her flashlight.

"Stop it!" I said, jumping away.

Heather laughed. "Boone rhymes with baboon." She poked me again.

"Ow. Be serious," I said. "I mean it."

Why did I ask her to come with me? I must have been out in the sun too long. My brain was fried or something!

The hissing cut out suddenly. The silence was eerie.

We leaned into the wind and started to climb. My flashlight beam darted around my feet.

The ground became soft and wet. My flip-flops squished as we climbed.

At the top of the hill, I could see a large, dark building, black against the purple sky.

The hissing began again. So close, the sound rang in my ears and made my *teeth* hurt!

What was that dark building above us? Was it filled with hissing snakes?

Heather and I would soon find out.

12

Our flashlights danced over the wet grass. The half-moon disappeared behind clouds. The building on the hilltop vanished in the darkness.

"Think Mom and Dad will at least send me a card?" Heather asked.

"Huh? A card? For *what*?" I asked.

"For my birthday. It's in two days," Heather said. "See? You forgot, too."

She gave me a hard shove that almost sent me tumbling down the hill. "I *told* you no one ever remembers my birthday."

"Could you please shut up?" I groaned. "Who *cares* about your birthday right now? We didn't sneak up here in the middle of the night to talk about your stupid birthday."

"You're stupid," she muttered.

She said something else, but I didn't hear it. The hissing rang so loudly in my ears, I could barely hear my own *thoughts*!

Hey, I'm a brave dude – but no lie, this was *scary*.

We reached the top of the hill. I was drenched in sweat. I wiped my forehead with the sleeve of my T-shirt.

The moon slid out from behind the clouds. Pale light swept over a long two-storey building. The windows were covered. No light escaped.

A tall hedge blocked the front of the building from view. I couldn't see an opening in the hedge.

The hissing cut off again. And now we stood in a deep silence.

Was anyone up here? Why did the hissing sound keep starting and stopping so suddenly?

"Follow me," I whispered to Heather. My heart was thumping like crazy in my chest. I lowered my shoulder and pushed my way through the hedge.

I turned and helped pull my sister through the thick, prickly branches. Then we stopped and studied the building.

"Is it somebody's house?" Heather whispered. "Does Dr Crawler live up here?"

"No," I said. "He lives in the little house behind the mess hall."

We stepped closer, into the deep shadows of the building. The front door was narrow, built of solid wood. The whole house stood as dark as a tomb.

I grabbed the doorknob and twisted it. I gave the door a tug.

Locked.

"All the other cabins and buildings have signs on them," Heather whispered.

"Maybe they want to keep this one a secret," I said.

I led the way around to the side. My flip-flops squished on the wet grass. A chill trickled down my body.

I knew we weren't supposed to be up there. But it was too late to go back.

Keeping close to the wall, we turned and crept slowly along the back of the house. "Heather, look—" I pointed to a dim orange glow up ahead.

We found the back door and peered in through a smeared glass window. I saw a narrow hallway. It was lit by a small lamp on the wall.

I tried the door.

Yes! Unlocked. I held it open for my sister. She hesitated for a moment. I saw a flash of fear on her face.

"Want to wait outside?" I whispered.

She stuck her tongue out at me.

My legs were shaking as I stepped into the hall. Warm inside. And silent.

I shut the door softly behind us. I waited for my eyes to adjust to the dim orange glow.

The hall led to a single door at the far end. No other doors or hallways.

"Let's see what's here," I whispered.

I took a deep breath and began to creep towards the door. The plank floorboards creaked under us. I tried to walk on tiptoe. But that isn't easy in flip-flops.

Any moment, I expected someone to come popping out that door and grab us.

But no. We made it to the far end of the hall.

I took a few seconds to catch my breath. Then, carefully . . . slowly . . . I pulled open the door.

Darkness on the other side. I couldn't see a thing.

Heather and I stepped into the room. Where were we?

We raised our flashlights – and gasped.

"They . . . they're ALIVE!" I cried.

13

I jumped back and hit the wall. I grabbed my sister and pulled her beside me.

The flashlight trembled in my hand. But I swept it back and forth over the room.

And stared in shock at the room filled with MICE.

Hundreds of them. In a pile nearly to the ceiling. No, not a pile. A *mountain* of mice.

Squeaking and chittering. A thousand tiny voices at once. Two thousand little black eyes . . . a thousand whipping tails.

They crawled over each other. They never stopped clawing and climbing. Struggling to climb to the top of the pile.

Their pink tails snapped and wriggled. Tiny jaws clamped open and shut.

I held the flashlight beam on the pile of living creatures. I couldn't take my eyes off the wild tangle of bodies.

Frozen against the wall, I watched them climb and scramble over each other and claw and bite, scratching and scraping.

"Oh!" Heather and I both uttered cries as a clump of mice fell off the pile and hit the floor with a hard *thud*.

Several landed on their backs. Their little paws kicked the air. And they swung back to their feet – and leaped back into the pile.

"I . . . I don't believe this," Heather stammered. "Boone, do they see us? What's keeping them in the centre of the room?"

I raised my beam of light. "They're in a cage. See?" I said. "It's like chicken wire. Very thin wire. Look. It goes up to the ceiling. They're totally caged in."

At the top of the mountain, several mice were nearly pressed against the ceiling. As other mice scrambled to the top, they lost their place and went toppling down the pile. Then they started their climb again from the bottom.

Heather's eyes were wide with fright. She pressed her hands against her cheeks. "Boone," she whispered, "all these mice. What are they *doing* here?"

She grabbed my arm and squeezed it. "I mean . . . what is *happening* here?"

I swallowed hard. I kept the light on the swarming, squeaking mice. "Serpo," I muttered.

Heather squeezed my arm tighter. "Excuse me? What did you just say?"

"Serpo," I repeated. "The big snake. The mice are here to feed him. They are food for Serpo. To keep him from attacking the camp."

Heather scrunched up her face. "Roddy's snake story? Boone, you're starting to believe his crazy story?"

I nodded. "Yes. I believe it. Looking at these mice, I believe it. This is a food pantry, Heather. For feeding Serpo, a giant snake."

"But, Boone—"

"I believe Roddy's story," I said. "I think they got rid of Roddy to keep him from telling the story to other campers. But I believe it. And . . . I believe we're all in real danger at this camp."

"I . . . don't know what to believe," Heather said in a trembling voice. "But these mice . . . they're too creepy. Let's get *out* of here!"

Keeping our backs against the wall, we slid towards the door. In front of us, the mountain of mice collapsed. The scramble to the top began again.

I reached the door. It was closed. I didn't remember closing it.

"Hurry," Heather whispered. "I . . . I need to get out of here."

I twisted the knob and pushed.

The door didn't budge.

I twisted it the other way. Pushed.

I leaned my shoulder into it and pushed hard.

No. Not moving.

I turned the knob and tried pulling. No.

"Boone – hurry!" Heather cried.

"The door is stuck," I said.

And then I felt something warm and scratchy on my ankle.

I kicked hard. But I felt prickly stabs on both legs. A warm body rubbed against my ankle.

I lowered the light. I saw a big tear in the wire cage. Mice were tumbling out through the opening. Pouring over the floor towards Heather and me.

I felt a mouse climb up my leg. Felt its warm, dry body. Felt its pinprick paws dig into my skin.

Two more crawled over my flip-flops.

Heather screamed. "Boone – help! They're *on* me! They're climbing up my *back*!"

I kicked a pack of mice off my feet. But four more scrambled around my ankles.

Heather twisted and squirmed. She shook her whole body, tossing mice into the air.

A mouse leaped on to my back. I ducked and spun and sent it flying.

"Ohhhh, help," Heather moaned. "They're swarming – more and more of them! They're going to *bury* us!"

I grabbed the doorknob. Twisted it. Pushed the door with all my strength. I frantically shook the knob back and forth.

Did we lock ourselves in?

Or did someone else lock the door?

My shoulder prickled. I felt something warm on my neck.

I pulled a mouse out of my hair and tossed it into the pile. I kicked one leg, then the other, trying to keep the squealing creatures off.

"What are we going to do? What are we going to *do*?" Heather shrieked. She plucked a mouse from her neck. I saw one slide off the back of her shorts.

"Is there another door?" I choked out. I bumped a mouse off my knee. It let out a squeal and jumped on to my foot.

I glanced all around. The room had only one door.

Mice were streaming out of the wire cage, across the floor. "Ow!" I felt a sharp bite on my arm. I felt prickly scratches up and down my legs.

They were *pouring* over Heather and me!

"They ... they're going to EAT us!" I stammered.

And the door swung open.

"Dr Crawler!" I cried.

We were *caught*!

No. Dim light from the hall slanted into the room. Two faces appeared. Sid and Kelly.

They both let out startled cries when they saw Heather and me battling the mice.

"I don't *believe* this!" Sid exclaimed. His eyes bulged. He stared at the mountain of scrambling mice.

Then he and Kelly dived into the room and began tugging mice off Heather and me. They flung them back towards the mountain, then grabbed us and yanked us out of the room.

The four of us stumbled out the door. I couldn't stop shivering and shuddering. I still had a mouse crawling up my neck.

Sid grabbed it and tossed it back into the room. Then I slammed the door shut.

Heather and I stood there in the narrow hall, unable to stop shaking. I hugged myself. But I couldn't stop chill after chill from sweeping down my back. All I could think of was jumping into a shower and staying under it for *hours*!

I knew I'd see that quivering, squealing mountain of mice in my dreams.

Sid and Kelly led the way out of the building. Heather and I gulped down breath after breath of fresh air.

Finally, I turned to my two bunkmates. "How did you find us?" I asked.

"We saw you sneak out of the cabin," Kelly replied. "So we followed you up the hill."

"That was totally freaky in there. What are those mice doing in that room?" Sid asked.

"Good question," I said.

The hissing sound started up again, so close it made us all jump.

"We've got to find out what this is about," Heather said. She fluffed out her hair with both hands. She smiled when she didn't find any mice.

"The counsellors know," Sid said. "They've *got* to."

"Let's wake them up," I said. I started to trot down the hill, slipping on the dewy grass.

"Yeah. Let's make 'em tell us the truth!" Heather cried.

The four of us half ran, half slid down the hill. The moon kept riding in and out behind clouds. Deep shadows swept over us, then faded in the moonlight.

Nathan and four other counsellors had their own cabin behind the arts and crafts cabin. We trotted up to the door.

The counsellors' cabin stood in deep shadows. The hissing from up on the hill suddenly stopped.

I pounded on the door.

"Hey – wake up!" Heather shouted.

I pounded again.

Silence. No one stirred.

"Let's go in," I said. I pulled open the screen door and stepped inside.

Heather, Sid and Kelly followed me in. The cabin was hot and stuffy and smelled of sweat.

"Yo! Wake up!" I said.

Silence. No one moved.

"Wow, these dudes are, like, out cold!" Sid whispered.

My eyes slowly adjusted to the darkness. I

could see two bunk beds against the wall and a cot under one window.

I stepped up to the cot. A long lump stretched under the bedsheet. One of the sleeping counsellors.

"Nathan? Is that you?" I whispered. "Wake up!"

I poked the sheet gently with two fingers.

The bedsheet moved. I jumped back as something slipped out from under the sheet.

At first, I thought I was looking at a fire hose. But it took me only a second to realize I was staring at a *huge snake*!

The snake uncoiled. Raised itself high – and snapped back its head, ready to attack.

15

I stumbled back. My breath caught in my throat.

The snake was a cottonmouth – venomous and deadly.

Its tongue darted out. Its tiny black eyes glowed, and it made an ugly hissing sound.

I tried to back out of the cabin. But I bumped into Kelly. We all pressed against the cabin wall.

Something moved in a top bunk. Then the sheets began to shift in both bunks. Snakes uncoiled. They rose up, pushing aside the bedsheets.

I saw several snakes in every bed. They had been coiled under the sheets. But now they climbed up, raised themselves, preparing to strike.

"Th-they're all poisonous!" I choked out. I pointed. "That's a copperhead. That's a rattlesnake."

"Where are the counsellors?" Heather cried in a tiny voice. "How did the snakes get into their beds?"

The rattler slid out of the bed and landed silently on the cabin floor. A copperhead dropped from the top bunk and slithered down.

The snakes had their eyes on us. They were coming after us!

I spun away and lowered my shoulder to the screen door. I shoved it open and burst out of the cabin.

Heather came running out next, her eyes wide with fright. Sid and Kelly were right behind her.

We didn't say a word. We just ran, slipping on the wet grass. Our feet thudded hard. The only other sound was our huffing breaths.

I turned and glanced back. "They're *following* us!" I gasped.

Yes. The snakes were wriggling rapidly through the tall grass. I could see their heads bobbing, dark eyes catching the glow of the pale moonlight.

Six of them. Some snapped their jaws as they slid through the grass. So fast. They were gliding so fast!

The moonlight made them shine like silver against the swaying grass. Silver monsters.

Sid and Kelly ran past me, on to the dirt trail

that led to our cabin. Heather fell behind.

"Hurry!" I shouted to her. Then I turned and chased after my two bunkmates.

A sharp pain cut into my side. I gasped and kept running. I could see our cabin up ahead. Would we be safe there?

One of my flip-flops caught on a tree root and flew off. I stumbled. Staggered forward to regain my balance.

And I heard a scream behind me: "HELP! HELP ME! IT GOT ME!"

Heather's scream!

I screeched to a stop. Swung around. And ran back towards my sister.

I could see her sprawled face down on the ground. She was kicking her legs hard, pounding the grass with both fists.

"Boone – help me!" she cried.

And then I saw the silvery snake wrapped around her ankle. And the other snakes wriggling close behind her.

"Stop moving! Freeze!" I shouted to her.

Then I dived to the ground. Landed hard on my knees.

I carefully wrapped my hand around the cottonmouth, grasping it tightly behind its head.

I lifted the head away from my sister's leg. Then slowly . . . slowly . . . I unwrapped the snake from her ankle.

Heather pushed herself up. She climbed quickly to her feet.

"Ohhhh," she moaned. "I don't believe this. I can still *feel* it on my leg!" Her whole body shuddered.

I lowered the cottonmouth to the ground and hurled it towards the other snakes. Then I grabbed Heather's hand and pulled her away.

She darted into her cabin. Then I ran to my cabin – one flip-flop off, one flip-flop on. Sid and Kelly were already inside. I slammed the door shut behind me.

They had their faces pressed against the cabin window. I pushed up between my two new friends and squinted out the window. I stared out on to the path. Shadows shifted. The moonlight faded.

No snakes.

We still hadn't said a word.

I shut my eyes and pictured those venomous snakes slowly unwinding in the counsellors' beds. Again, I saw the sheets move and those snakes rise up, angry that we had awakened them.

"Too weird," I muttered. "It's all too weird."

Sid and Kelly nodded their heads. Their faces were tight with fear.

My chest felt fluttery. My body was covered in a cold sweat.

"Tomorrow," I said. "Tomorrow at breakfast, I'm going to find Nathan. I'm going to force him to talk. I'm going to make him tell us what's up with this camp."

*   *   *

We saw Nathan *before* breakfast. He came into
the cabin and woke us up by playing a kazoo in
our ears.

Yawning, I glanced out the window. The sun
was just rising over the trees.

"Rise and shine!" Nathan chanted. "Rise and
shine, guys!" He began spraying us with Sun-
Glo.

I dropped to the floor. My pyjama bottoms
were all twisted. I shielded my eyes from the
spray. "Give me a break!" I shouted.

Nathan laughed. He started tooting his kazoo
again.

I grabbed it away from him. "We've got to talk
to you," I said.

His grin faded. "What's your problem, dude?"

"We went to your cabin last night," Sid said.
"Where were you?"

"Yeah, where were the counsellors?" I
demanded. "Your cabin was filled with snakes."

"Poisonous snakes," Kelly said.

The three of us surrounded him. We stood
with our fists on our hips, watching him, waiting
for answers.

Nathan blinked. "Take a breath," he said.
"What were you guys doing out last night?"

"Just answer our questions," I said.

"I don't know anything about snakes," Nathan

67

said. "We were camping. All the counsellors. We slept in tents down by the lake."

I stared at him. Was he lying?

"It's a tradition," Nathan said. "The counsellors always have a campout the first week of camp."

I poked the plastic kazoo into Nathan's stomach. "But what about the snakes sleeping in your beds?" I demanded.

He shrugged. "I don't know. I don't understand it. Guess they saw an empty cabin. So they jumped at the chance for a warm bed."

He's totally lying, I decided.

"Nathan, we're not stupid. They were all venomous snakes. Even pit vipers," I said. "All deadly. They didn't just sneak into your cabin because it was empty."

Nathan shrugged again. "I just went to my cabin to change. I didn't see any snakes." He laughed. "You sure you little boys didn't have a scary nightmare?" he asked in a babyish voice.

"*All* of us?" Kelly cried. "You think we all had the same nightmare?"

"Beats me," Nathan said. "Really. I was in a tent all night. I don't know anything about snakes."

I balled my hands into tight fists. He was definitely lying. How could I get him to tell us the truth?

68

Maybe we should follow Roddy's example, I suddenly thought. *Maybe we should get out of this camp as fast as we can.*

Nathan grabbed the kazoo out of my hand. "Get dressed, dudes," he said. "Stop staring at me like frightened rabbits. Wear your swimming trunks to breakfast."

"Swimming trunks? Why?" I asked.

"This morning, you guys are going to practise for Cabin Wars. You're going to swim across the lake," Nathan said.

Nathan ran out of the cabin before we could say anything more.

"What about all the mice?" Kelly asked me. "Up on the hill. We didn't ask Nathan about the mice."

"He's not going to tell us the truth," I said. "He was lying about the snakes." I shook my head. "Also, we don't want him to know we were sneaking around up there. We can't trust him."

"What are we going to do?" Sid asked. "Now he's going to make us swim across the lake. I heard Roddy's story. About Serpo. About how they feed the giant snake."

I pulled my mobile phone from my backpack. "I think we have to get out of this camp," I said. "I'm calling home."

I started to punch in our number at home. But the silence made me stop. I stared at the phone: NO SERVICE.

Sid had a phone, too. He checked it. Same story. It didn't work.

We pulled on our swimming trunks and went to breakfast. They had biscuits and gravy. I filled my plate, but then I couldn't eat anything.

Sid, Kelly and I were at our usual table. The counsellors sat at a long table in front of the kitchen. Were they staring at us?

Yes.

They kept watching us while they talked and ate. Why were they keeping such a close eye on the three of us?

I didn't like it.

There were a *lot* of things not to like. Serpo ... the room crammed with swarming mice ... the lake ... the venomous snakes in the cabin last night ... chasing us ... hunting us...

I pictured poor, frightened Roddy. Was he right about this camp?

Camp SLITHER.

Kids call this place Camp Slither.

Because it's CRAWLING with snakes?

Those mice... They have to be food for Serpo.

But are we food for Serpo, too?

I didn't even take one bite of my breakfast. I crossed the room to Heather's table. She had dark rings under her eyes. I could tell she hadn't been able to sleep.

She was talking to two other girls. I leaned

71

over her shoulder and whispered. "We have to get out of this camp," I said. "We're not safe here."

She nodded. "Should I tell my friends?"

"Yes," I said. "I think we're all in danger."

After breakfast, the counsellors were called to the main office for a short meeting. Outside the mess hall, I gathered my two bunkmates and some guys from other cabins. Heather brought her two friends.

"We've got to figure out the best way to escape," I said. "The lake is on that side." I pointed. "And we're surrounded by woods. So how do we get to a highway? Or a town?"

"Well, we can't swim for it!" one of her friends said.

"Oh, wait!" Heather cried. "I might have a map."

"Right," I said. "There was a map in the camp brochure. Did you bring it?"

Heather nodded. "I think it's tucked in the bottom of my camp trunk."

We followed Heather to Rattler, her cabin. She slid out her trunk and began tearing through it.

"Here it is!" She pulled out the camp brochure.

I grabbed it out of her hand. "Let me see the map."

I started to unfold it. But something caught my eye.

"Whoa! Wait!" I cried. "I *knew* something was

terribly wrong here."

I pointed to the back of the brochure. "Check this out."

Everyone gathered close. I read it to them:

"*If you have any problems at all, come see me. My door is always open. Sincerely, Uncle Jerry Landers, Head Counsellor.*'"

"Huh?" Heather's mouth dropped open. "Who is Uncle Jerry?"

Sid grabbed the brochure and studied it. "The head counsellor is someone named Uncle Jerry? Why haven't we seen him?"

"Don't you get it? This means that Dr Crawler isn't the real head counsellor," I said, my heart suddenly pounding. "Dr Crawler is some kind of fake."

The kids all started talking at once. I could see that everyone was scared and confused.

Heather and I finally got them all quiet.

"I'll bet Dr Crawler has done something to Uncle Jerry," Heather said. "I mean, like, Dr Crawler is this evil guy who likes to feed kids to snakes, right? I'll ding-dong bet you he's kidnapped Uncle Jerry or something."

"Sounds like a scary movie I saw," Kelly said.

"Yeah, it sounds totally crazy," I said. "But what if it's true?"

"How do we find out?" Sid asked.

"Simple. We try to find Uncle Jerry," I said.

18

We split up. Our plan was to search every building until we found a clue.

Heather and I headed to the small building behind the main lodge at the edge of the woods. We knew that Dr Crawler had his office there.

Was he hiding Uncle Jerry somewhere in that building?

A sign at the front door read: STAFF ONLY. CAMPERS KEEP OUT.

My chest felt a little fluttery, and my legs were trembling. I don't like going places where I don't belong.

But this was an emergency. Something was terribly wrong at Camp Hither.

We pushed open the front door and crept inside. We stood in a narrow wood-panelled hallway. Office doors on both sides.

The office doors were all closed. The building was silent.

"I think Dr Crawler is still at the counsellors' meeting," Heather whispered.

"Good," I said. Carefully, slowly, I pushed open the first office door. I saw a lot of filing cabinets and a desk piled high with folders.

We moved down the hall, opening the doors and peeking inside. The offices were all dark and empty.

"No one in this building," Heather whispered. "Everyone's outside."

I pointed to the stairway at the end of the hall. "We have to check upstairs," I said. My voice cracked. I wanted to get out of there.

We made our way up the wooden stairs as quietly as we could. The air was hot up there, and the hall was narrow and dimly lit.

I saw one closed door, almost hidden in shadow. Our footsteps echoed off the hardwood floor.

The door had a name stencilled on it in black. It read: UNCLE JERRY.

Heather and I exchanged glances. My hand trembled as I reached for the doorknob. I started to turn it, then stopped.

I knocked on the door instead.

We both gasped when a voice inside called, "Come in!"

I froze. "Is . . . is that you, Uncle Jerry?" I stammered.

"Yes. Come in!"

I took a deep breath. Turned the knob. Pushed open the door.

Heather and I both let out startled cries.

Dr Crawler grinned at us from behind the desk.

His eyes flashed and his grin grew wider, until I could see all his teeth. And they were *pointed*!

"Come in, come in," he said, waving us in.

Should we run away?

Not if we want to get to the bottom of this.

We stepped into the office.

There were two chairs behind the wide black steel desk. Dr Crawler sat in one, his long fingers tapping the desk. The other chair faced away from us.

I cleared my throat. "We . . . we . . . were looking for Uncle Jerry," I choked out.

Dr Crawler nodded. "Boone, Heather, good work. You've found him," he said.

I squinted at him. "Excuse me? We found him? Where?"

"Right here," Dr Crawler said.

He spun the other chair around.

My sister and I both jumped back when we saw the enormous cottonmouth snake coiled in the chair.

"Don't be scared, guys," Dr Crawler said. "This is Uncle Jerry!"

I swallowed hard. Beside me, Heather backed up towards the office door.

The snake tilted its head as if studying us. Its tongue licked the corners of its mouth.

"Uncle Jerry c-can't be a snake!" I stammered. I balled my hands into fists.

Dr Crawler grinned his pointy-toothed smile. "Would I lie to you, Boone?"

The snake arched its head, rose up taller in the chair, and opened its mouth with a long *hisssssss.*

"Boone, let's go," Heather whispered from behind me.

"No. I want to know the truth," I told her.

Sure, I was scared. So scared I could barely breathe.

But I was angry, too. I had to know what was really going on in this camp. Was Roddy right about *everything*?

"Uncle Jerry had a little accident in the lab," Dr Crawler said. "But I don't want you kids to worry. I'm taking very good care of him. And the others."

Others?

The big cottonmouth in the chair snapped its jaws.

And suddenly I just lost it. I let out a scream and dived forward.

I grabbed Dr Crawler by the arms. And I started shouting:

"Tell us the truth! Tell us the truth!"

I shook him hard. He tried to pull back. But I held on tight. And something happened. Something *slid* in my hands.

It took me a long while to realize it was his *skin*!

Dr Crawler's skin began to slide off.

As I tugged his arms, the skin pulled out from his shirtsleeves. It felt kind of like shrink wrap. Only it was flaky and dry. And warm.

I tried to let go. But the skin stuck to my hands.

I choked and started to gag.

I staggered back. More skin rolled off his body. Off his face. . . His chest. . .

Dr Crawler was shedding his skin like a snake!

I stood there gasping. And as the skin came

off in my hands, I saw that his human body wasn't real.

His clothing collapsed in a heap on the floor. His body started to shrink. I watched in horror as his head, his arms, his legs vanished.

A few seconds later, Dr Crawler was gone. And a long, hissing snake crawled out from one of his trouser legs.

A copperhead snake.

Heather and I stood frozen. Now there were *two* snakes in front of us.

The skin dropped from my hands and spilled silently to the floor.

"You sssshouldn't have done that," Uncle Jerry hissed.

"Y-you can SPEAK!" I gasped.

"My brain is human," Uncle Jerry replied in a dry whisper that sounded like crackling leaves. "I can sspeak . . . and I can BITE!"

"Now we have no choisssssse," Dr Crawler uttered.

"Boone – let's GO!" Heather screamed.

I turned to run. But the doorway filled with snakes. Six or seven poisonous snakes, coiling and curling on each other. Blocking our escape.

"Don't try anything foolissshhhhh," Dr Crawler hissed. "Their bite is sharp. And their poison works in seconds!"

20

Nathan and the other counsellors appeared in the doorway. They stepped over the knot of snakes. They didn't say a word.

The counsellors forced us outside and up the hill. To the low building we had seen the night before.

Dr Crawler, Uncle Jerry and the other snakes slithered beside us, pulling themselves silently through the tall grass.

"Our lab was here for many years," Dr Crawler said.

"We were ssssssscientists studying sssssnake venom," Uncle Jerry hissed. "We were trying to find antidotes. Ways to cure the poison. We injected ourselves and the young people who worked for us. But we made a terrible missssstake."

"We wanted to be famousssss," Dr Crawler said in a crackling whisper. "Sssso we injected ourselves too ssssoooon. We all became ssssnakes."

"We're trying to reverse it all," Dr Crawler said. "Ssssome of us are almost back to normal. Ssssome of usss become human in the daytime. But it wears off by night. At night, we become sssssnakes again."

Heather and I both gasped. The counsellors' cabin. Those snakes in the beds. They were Nathan and the other counsellors! Humans who turned into snakes at night!

"What about Serpo?" I cried. "Is that true, too?"

"Sssserpo?" Uncle Jerry hissed. "That's a sssstupid old legend. Who would believe a sssstory like that?"

"But – all the mice. . .?" I said.

The two snakes flicked their tongues. "We have to *eat*, don't we?"

"Why are you taking us up here?" Heather cried. "What are you going to do to us?"

"We need you in the lab," Dr Crawler said. "We don't want to sssstay sssssnakes for ever."

"We need fresh humans to do our tests on," Uncle Jerry added. "That's why we sssstarted this camp. We need to experiment – to find the right formula to make us human again."

"Experiment?" I cried.

"Yes. And we have to do it fast," Dr Crawler said. "The townspeople have been getting ssssuspicious. Too many questions. The police will be closing in on us soon. So we have to *act*!"

We reached the top of the hill. The long building came into view. Nathan and the other counsellors shoved us forward.

The hissing sound started up again, so loud I covered my ears.

"What *is* that?" I cried. "Tell me the truth! What is that hissing sound?"

"You'll soon find out," Nathan murmured. "Real soon."

He and the other counsellors pushed us through the front door. We stepped into a large science lab.

Enormous machines lined the walls, humming loudly. The ceiling was covered with tangled cords and cables. A dozen computer screens blinked and flickered. Against one wall, metal cones hung down on long cords from the ceiling.

The machines began to hiss, as if letting out steam.

I turned to my sister. "Heather," I said, shouting over the noise. "The hissing we heard. It *wasn't* snakes. It was these machines!"

The snakes crawled over each other, forming a tight knot, guarding the door. The counsellors pushed us across the huge room.

"Just cooperate," Nathan whispered. "Maybe you'll end up in the same body you started with."

Huh? Those words sent a cold shiver down my back.

Against the far wall, I saw a boy. He had a metal cone pulled down on his head.

As we walked closer, I recognized the boy. "Roddy!" I shouted. "Roddy! You're *here*!"

Roddy turned to us. He opened his mouth to speak.

And Heather and I both uttered horrified cries.

Roddy had a thin, black, forked tongue.

21

The counsellors surrounded us. Dr Crawler slithered in front of Roddy. "This boy is helping ussss," he said. "And now you will, too. I've been preparing you sssssince you arrived."

"Preparing us?" I cried. "What do you mean?"

Dr Crawler's shiny snake eyes flashed with excitement. "The Ssssun-Glo sssspray isn't ssssun protection," he said. "It's snake DNA."

"Your ssskin is sssssoaked with it," Uncle Jerry said. "Now let's sssssee if we can find the right power level to transform you into sssssnakes."

"Transform us into snakes?" Heather cried. "Why?"

"We need to change you into poisonous sssssnakes so that we can figure out how to change you back into humans," Uncle Jerry said. "If we can change *you* back to humans, we'll know how to change *ourselves* back to humans!"

My whole body shuddered. What would it *feel* like to be a snake?

I didn't want to find out. I lowered my head like a rugby player – and took off.

I got about four steps. Nathan tackled me and brought me down to the floor. Snakes slithered over and wrapped themselves around my legs.

When I looked up, counsellors had already pulled a metal cone over Heather's head.

I couldn't escape. I couldn't help her. The counsellors pushed me to the wall between Roddy and my sister. They fastened a metal cone over my head.

"It doesn't hurt," Nathan whispered.

"But I don't *want* to be a snake!" I screamed.

"Neither do I," he muttered. He pulled the metal cone lower on my head.

Uncle Jerry slithered in front of us. "The big hissing machines ssssend the power into the metal cones. The power works with the ssssnake DNA to change you."

"Your friend Roddy is already helping ussss," Dr Crawler hissed. He turned to Uncle Jerry. "Let's sssssee if we have any ssssuccess with him today."

"No – don't hurt him!" I shouted. "Don't do it – please!"

The hissing grew to a deafening roar. It sounded like a hundred fire hoses going off at once.

Nathan crossed the lab to a huge control panel. He threw a switch.

Roddy let out a groan. His black snake tongue flicked in and out.

His knees collapsed. His body started to twitch and vibrate. Bright white and yellow sparks shot out of the helmet.

"Stop it! STOP IT!" Heather and I both screamed.

I gaped in horror as Roddy's body appeared to melt away. He melted right out of his clothes.

A few seconds later, he was a snake – a long yellow snake with bright red stripes – crawling on the floor in front of us!

22

"Ssssuccess!" Dr Crawler cried. He raised himself tall and did a kind of shuffling snake dance.

"We are doing well today," Uncle Jerry agreed. "Getting very close. Ssssoon you will be ssssnakes, too. Ssssnakes we can try to change back to humans."

"You can't *do* this!" Heather screamed. "Let us go! You cannot get away with this!"

Roddy – now a long, thick snake – crawled over the floor towards my sister and me. I watched him move, studying his red-and-yellow stripe pattern.

"Let'ssss try you next, Boone," Dr Crawler hissed. He bobbed his head towards Nathan.

"No – please!" I cried. "Please—"

Once again, Nathan threw a switch.

I felt the cone over my head start to vibrate. My head began to tingle. My eyes blurred. My whole body throbbed as if I had stuck my finger in an electrical socket.

Last chance, Boone, I told myself. *Last chance before you become a snake. . .*

I signalled to my sister. I pointed frantically.

Yes. After a few seconds, she understood me. Heather raised her arm – and *rattled* her bracelet as hard as she could.

The sound startled Dr Crawler and Uncle Jerry. I saw their heads whip around.

It gave me *one second* to move. I tore off the vibrating cone and dived to the floor. I grabbed Roddy. The big snake wriggled in my hands. I raised it high over my head.

Dr Crawler's eyes flashed. "What are you doing with that sssssnake?" he hissed.

I held the snake high. "Do you know the biggest predators of snakes?" I demanded. "Do you know the two biggest *enemies* of snakes?"

Dr Crawler pulled his head back. "I know that *man* is the firsssst," he replied. "Humans are the biggest enemy of sssssnakes."

"And the *second* biggest enemy?" I cried. "You should know this!"

The two startled snakes stared at me.

"The king snake is the second biggest enemy," I told them. "King snakes *love* to eat other snakes. And guess what? You just turned Roddy into a king snake!"

I didn't give them a chance to move. I heaved the king snake on to Dr Crawler.

Dr Crawler arched his head. He tried to squirm away.

The king snake let out a warning hiss.

But Dr Crawler opened his jaws – and attacked first. His head darted forward as he snapped at Roddy's throat.

Roddy pulled his head back.

Dr Crawler missed – *and accidentally bit HIMSELF*!

Heather pulled herself free of the metal cone. We both watched as the venom instantly shot through Dr Crawler's body.

"He poisoned *himself*!" Heather cried.

Dr Crawler slumped heavily to the floor. He didn't move.

The counsellors uttered cries of shock and horror. Uncle Jerry stared down at Dr Crawler, then started for the door. The snakes all began to hiss at once.

And then they all turned and, wriggling and slithering furiously, followed Uncle Jerry out of the lab.

I watched them fleeing down the hill. Their leader was dead. They were defeated.

I turned to Heather – and uttered a shocked cry. Roddy stood beside her, looking like his old, human self.

He shook his head, confused. "I'm a little dizzy," he said.

"I guess Dr Crawler's experiment was a failure," I said. "It only lasted for five minutes."

"Five minutes was plenty," Roddy said. "I *told* you this camp was creepy! Look at me. I'm all dusty from crawling on the floor! Yuck! Next summer, I'm going to *Latin* camp!"

23

A happy ending for everyone but the snakes.

The next day, Mom and Dad picked us up. We tried to explain why camp closed early. We told them the whole story. But I don't think they believed us.

Who *would*?

Heather and I sat in the back seat, watching the trees speed by, happy to be going home.

"Why do you have that grin on your face?" Heather asked.

"I'll show you," I said. I reached into my backpack. I pulled out a little garden snake. I handed it to my sister.

"What's this, Boone?" Heather asked.

"A present," I said. "You never shut up about how no one remembered your birthday. So I picked it up for you this morning. Happy birthday!"

She stared at it. "For my birthday? Are

you *crazy*?"

And before I could answer, the snake opened its jaws and hissed, "Many happy returnsss!"

ENTER
HORRORLAND

THE STORY SO FAR...

A group of kids received invitations to be Very Special Guests at a scary theme park called HorrorLand. They came looking for good, creepy fun – but instead, they found real horror.

Frightening villains from their pasts followed them to the park. A park worker, a Horror called Byron, warned them they weren't safe in HorrorLand. He said their lives were in danger.

After three kids in their group mysteriously disappeared, the Very Special Guests decided to escape. They made it as far as the car park. It didn't take long to realize they had walked into a trap.

Boone Dixon continues the story. . .

1

I thought I'd be spending the whole summer at Camp Hither. But one week later, I was happy to be away from that horrible place. Happy to be home. But it wasn't all good. My sister was driving me crazy.

Heather wanted to play croquet in the back garden all day. And she *cheated* at it! Can you imagine a kid so *lame* she cheats at croquet?

My friends were all away. And every morning, Mom and Dad took turns saying, "Boone, have you done your summer reading yet?"

Wow. Awesome summer, huh? And I didn't even mention the nightmares about snakes almost every night.

So when the invitation came from HorrorLand Theme Park, I was *psyched*.

The card had a grinning monster on the front. At the park, I think they call them Horrors. And under the monster, in creepy, blood-red lettering, my name: Boone Dixon.

An invitation for a whole week at HorrorLand as a Very Special Guest.

The scariest theme park on earth. Could I say no?

Mom and Dad put me on the bus two days later. As the towns, farms and forests passed by my window, I couldn't stop thinking about the great rides and shows and scary fun.

I knew where I wanted to go first. My friend Jonathan had told me all about Werewolf Village. He swore the werewolves there were *real*.

I knew he had to be joking. But if you know me, you know I don't like mysteries. I had to check it out for myself.

The bus ride was four hours. I was too excited to sit still. I kept getting up and changing seats.

Finally, the driver braked the bus and shouted, "HorrorLand Park. This is as close as I go."

I peered out the window. I was at the entrance to the huge car park. I pulled my bag from the overhead rack. And I stepped down from the bus.

The bus pulled away with a roar. I shielded my eyes from the bright sunlight. The car park was jammed with row after row of cars. Under the blazing sun, the cars all glowed as if they were on fire.

I could see the park entrance at the other end

of the car park. A tall green-and-purple fence surrounded the park.

I shifted the bag to my other hand. Then I began making my way through the long rows of cars.

As I got closer to the park, I could see the top of a black roller coaster near the fence. And I could hear screams and laughs and creepy music blaring.

Two ticket booths stood at the front entrance. I pulled out my invitation. And I started to trot towards the gate.

But then I stopped.

I saw a group of kids near the entrance. There were about eight or nine of them. At first, I thought they were playing with some kind of net.

Then I heard their screams. And I realized they were *struggling* against the net.

Were they trapped under it?

Yes! Screaming and crying out for help, they thrashed and kicked and tried to free themselves.

I dropped my bag on the asphalt. I started towards them – and gasped!

I blinked. I struggled to focus my eyes in the blinding sunlight.

I stood there, staring. It wasn't a net.

It was *snakes*. The kids were covered in SNAKES!

I froze. My breath caught in my throat. It all came rushing back to me. All the terrifying, poisonous snakes I had just escaped from. . .

"HELP US!"

"SOMEBODY – HELP!"

The kids' screams jolted me from my panic. My heart pounding, I ran to see if I could help.

A few metres away, I realized I was wrong. I *wasn't* staring at snakes.

The kids were trapped inside a web of long purple vines. The vines had twisted all around them. They were trapped together – and the vines were *moving*!

I could see the long tendrils growing . . . curling around the struggling kids. Tightening around them.

I couldn't believe my eyes. How was this *possible*?

"HELP US!"

"I . . . CAN'T . . . BREATHE. . ."

A girl stretched her arm out towards me. The purple tendrils quickly wrapped around her wrist. "Help . . . me. . ."

"OK! I'll try!" I shouted.

I dived forward and grabbed the vine around her arm. I tugged it with all my strength. I wanted to rip it away.

The girl let out a shrill howl of pain.

"STOP!" she screamed. "Don't pull it! It's growing FROM me!"

"Huh?" I gasped. I dropped the vine and stumbled back a step.

I peered in through the thick tendrils. I could just see the girl's eyes. "What do you mean?" I said. "I . . . don't understand."

"The vines . . . they're growing out of our HANDS!" the girl wailed. "They're . . . attached to us!"

I didn't know what to think. Was this really *happening*?

The girl screamed in pain again. The others shouted for help.

I decided it was real.

I grabbed the vine around the girl's arm again. "I'll be more careful," I said.

I tried to slide it away from her arm. I was being very gentle. I unwrapped a few

101

centimetres of it. But the tendrils were tangled and twisted together.

I worked at it for a minute or two. "Can you slide your arm out?" I asked her.

"No. It's still tangled," she said.

Kids were squirming and thrashing beneath the vines.

Suddenly, I felt something move around my waist. I glanced down – and let out a horrified gasp.

A vine had wrapped around my middle.

"No! No!" I cried. I tried to jerk free. But the vine closed around me – and pulled me in with the other kids.

I grabbed it with both hands. But before I could tug it off me, another vine curled around my neck.

The vines were warm, and they were dry, like snakes. They moved quickly, curling and choking me.

Trapped. I couldn't even struggle against them.

Tightening . . . tightening . . . they pulled me down.

3

I dropped to my knees. I couldn't pull them off. And I couldn't twist away from them.

I tried *biting* one – and heard a boy scream.

Were the vines really growing from the kids? It was too creepy to think about.

"Unnnh." I let out a groan as the tendrils pulled me down to the asphalt.

Kids screamed and moaned. And then their cries were drowned out by a roar.

I glanced out from the net of vines. The roar came from a purple bus. It pulled up beside us and stopped with a squeal of brakes.

A green-and-purple monster jumped off the bus. He was short and thin and had tiny stubs of horns growing from the top of his head. I guessed he was a Horror.

He walked up to the net of vines and stood with his furry paws on his waist. Four bigger Horrors lumbered up behind him. They were muscular and nasty looking and scowled down at us.

The kids all grew silent. No one moved. The vines continued to slide and curl.

"That Horror . . . it's Ned," a girl whispered to the others. "Remember him? Ned?"

"I'm so sorry you Very Special Guests tried to leave the park," Ned said. His voice was soft. He didn't sound like a monster. He sounded like my English teacher.

"Let us out!" a boy cried.

"We're suffocating!" another boy shouted. "Can't breathe!"

"It hurts! It's too tight!"

"You brought this on yourselves," Ned said. "You gave us no choice."

"Let us out!"

"You can't DO this!"

One of the big Horrors handed Ned a tool. It was silvery and had a wide bell at the top, then a handle with a trigger. It looked a little like a hair dryer.

"I'm going to free you now," Ned said. "Don't anyone try to run away. I need you to return to the park."

He pushed the trigger on the handle. The silvery tool started to whir. He aimed it at the vine around my throat.

I felt the vine loosen. It instantly shrank.

I took a long, deep breath.

Ned moved the whirring tool from vine to vine. The tendrils slid off the kids and quickly vanished.

Two boys jumped to their feet. They scratched their hands. They took deep breaths and gazed around.

A big Horror moved close to them. He stood with his muscles tensed. Alert. He wasn't going to let the two boys try to escape.

A short while later, the kids were all on their feet. They were stretching their arms and taking deep breaths and rubbing the backs of their hands.

"On to the bus!" one of the Horrors boomed. The big Horrors started shoving kids on to the purple bus.

Ned handed the silvery tool to a Horror. I stepped up to him. He studied me. "You're new?" he asked.

I nodded. "Yes. I don't belong with this group."

He frowned at me. "Really?"

"I . . . I just came over to help them," I said. "I thought they were being attacked by snakes."

"Snakes?" a big Horror cried.

"Did he say he saw *snakes*?"

The Horrors all spun around to stare at me.

"I'm *terrified* of snakes," I heard one Horror

mutter to the Horror next to him.

"Me, too," his partner whispered.

"Let's not talk about snakes," Ned said to me.

"OK, OK," I said. "But look. I just got here. I . . . I have this invitation."

I pulled the card out of my jeans pocket. "I just got off the bus. Two minutes ago."

"Boone Dixon." Ned read my name on the invitation.

His eyes narrowed as he handed it back to me. He grabbed my bag in one furry paw. "Well, guess what, Boone," he said. "You DO belong with the others. Get on the bus – *now*!"

4

Two big Horrors moved towards me, flexing their muscles. I had no choice. I turned and climbed on to the bus.

My head was spinning. What was going on here? I thought HorrorLand was a place to have fun. These other kids were Very Special Guests, too.

Why were they being treated like prisoners?

The bus was old and beat-up inside. Some of the seats were ripped. The bus smelled like sweat and ripe fruit.

I found a seat in the third row next to a dark-haired boy about my age. He told me his name – Matt Daniels. Then he introduced the two girls in the seat in front of us. Carly Beth and Sabrina. He pointed out a brother and sister across from us – Billy and Sheena Deep.

So many kids. I struggled to keep the names straight.

"What's going on?" I asked Matt.

He sighed. "It's a long story, Boone."

All the kids were on the bus now. The big Horrors squeezed in. One of them dropped into the driver's seat. The others took seats in the back. They were so heavy, the bus bounced when they sat down.

Ned stood at the front, holding on to a pole. He motioned for the Horror to start the bus.

The engine roared. The bus moved forward with a hard jolt. Ned grabbed the pole with his other paw to keep from falling into the aisle.

The bus turned out of the car park and sped through the entrance gate into the park. I saw several startled people leap out of the way.

"Where are we going?" Matt shouted to Ned. "Where are you taking us?"

"You need to stay in the park," Ned replied. The bus hit a bump, and he bumped with it. "I can't have you wandering off on your own."

"You can't keep us here against our will!" Carly Beth cried.

"I only want to keep you safe," Ned replied.

"Safe? Did you say *safe*?" Matt jumped to his feet. "Three kids have disappeared! Gone – just like that."

"Where are they? What happened to them?" Billy demanded.

"Calm down, everyone," Ned said. "We're looking for those kids. We don't want you to worry about them. Those kids aren't in any danger. Take my word."

"Take your word?" a boy shouted from the back. "Why should we take your word?"

"Where are Molly, Britney and Michael?" Sabrina asked. "Tell us!"

"Let us talk to Byron," Matt said, still standing. "Bring us to Byron. Let him explain."

"Yeah. Byron is our friend," Billy said.

Ned shook his head slowly. "Byron no longer works for the park," he said.

There were shocked cries all over the bus.

"We were very sorry to lose him," Ned said. "Very sorry indeed."

I watched the park roll by outside the window. I saw a theatre and a row of small shops. A sign read: WELCOME TO ZOMBIE PLAZA.

I was totally confused.

Byron? Missing kids? What were they talking about? I didn't have a clue.

Why were these kids so upset and angry?

Carly Beth jumped to her feet and jabbed a finger at Ned. "I have some questions for you," she said.

"I'll try to answer them," Ned replied.

"Tell us about Panic Park," Carly Beth said. "What is it? Where is it? And tell us why there are no mirrors in HorrorLand."

"I'm sorry," Ned said. "I'm happy to answer all your questions. Really, I am. But what you are asking about will take a long time to explain."

"Tell us!" Matt demanded. "Tell us the answers. We don't care how long it takes."

"Tell us! Tell us!" Kids started to chant.

Ned raised a hand to stop them. "The most important thing," he said, "is to keep you here in the park. To keep you away from harm."

Harm? What kind of harm?

"I just got here," I said. "Five minutes ago. I'm totally confused. Where are you taking us?"

"Where am I taking you? You've given me no choice," Ned replied.

He tightened his grip on the pole and leaned closer to us.

"I didn't want to do this," Ned said. "But I have to take you all to . . . The Keeper!"

Everyone began to shout and argue.

I watched them, trying to figure out what they were talking about.

Was Ned *crazy*?

He waved both paws to get everyone quiet. "I'm very sorry it has come to this," he said. "The Keeper's methods are . . . harsh. He can be unpleasant."

Ned shook his head. "Sorry," he said softly. "You have given me no choice."

Next to me, Matt was still on his feet. He ignored the bounces and bumps of the bus. He kept his eyes on Ned.

"How long do you think you can keep us prisoners here?" Matt demanded.

"You are not prisoners. You are Very Special Guests," Ned replied.

The kids all laughed scornfully.

"I need to keep you here until we know you

are safe from certain . . . things."

"What things?" Matt cried.

Ned ignored the question. "When it is safe we will return you to your parents," he said.

"It's not true!" Sheena Deep shouted. "Byron warned us we're not safe in HorrorLand!"

Her brother, Billy, jumped up. "If this park was safe, you wouldn't have to hold us prisoner!"

"Do not try to fight this," Ned said softly. "I'm giving you fair warning. Do not anger The Keeper. He can be . . . *difficult*."

That got all the kids shouting again.

I glanced out the window. The bus passed a fenced-in area of tall trees. A sign read: WEREWOLF VILLAGE.

I wanted out. I had come here to have fun. I felt as frightened as the others, even though I didn't really know what was happening.

Suddenly, I had an idea. A crazy idea to help us all escape from this weirdo, Ned.

Would it work?

"SNAKE!" I screamed. "SNAKE! On the bus!"

I ducked behind the seat and pretended to wrestle with it.

I grunted and groaned and pretended it was putting up a big battle.

"HELP!" I screamed. "This snake is HUGE! Help me!"

I had overheard the Horrors say they were terrified of snakes. Was it true?

Yes!

The bus squealed to a hard stop. So hard, Ned toppled forward into the first seat. And two kids were bounced off their seats on to the floor.

"SNAKE!" I cried. I kept pretending to struggle against it.

I saw the big bus driver jump up. His eyes were wide with fright. He was the first one off the bus.

Ned leaped off right after him. The other big

Horrors lumbered full speed up the aisle and jumped to the ground. Through the bus window, I watched them run off into the crowds.

I turned. Kids were frozen in their seats, frightened, too.

"No snake!" I shouted, jumping to my feet. "There's no snake. Let's get out of here!"

Matt slapped me a high five. "New kid – good work!" he cried. He spun around to the others. "This is our chance. Let's MOVE!"

We shoved our way down the narrow aisle and jumped off the bus. Matt led us behind it, where the Horrors wouldn't see us.

Across from us, I saw a line of people in front of a booth called THE PRETZEL PAL. A sign read: TURN YOURSELF INTO A PRETZEL! IT'S EASY!

It didn't sound like much fun to me.

The kids all huddled in the shadow of the bus.

"Which way?" a tall, dark-haired boy asked. "Have we been here before?"

A girl with two cameras around her neck pointed. "I think the entrance gates are that way."

"Then we want to go the other way," Sheena said. "We don't want to try *that* again."

"We've got to decide fast," I said. "Those Horrors will be back!"

Matt was studying a sign to our left. "Look – that's Goodbye Land," he said.

I turned. The sign was a big tombstone. Engraved on it were the words: GOODBYE LAND. WAVE GOODBYE TO YOUR FRIENDS & FAMILY.

"Remember?" Matt said. "Michael Munroe was leading us there – before he disappeared."

Everyone turned to stare at the tombstone. We couldn't see into Goodbye Land because it was bordered by a tall hedge.

"Michael said this was the back end of the park," Carly Beth said. "He thought there might be an exit there."

We all jumped as a siren began to wail.

"Hurry," Matt said, glancing around. "They set off the alarm. Telling the other Horrors that we've escaped."

We took off, running towards the entrance to Goodbye Land. But we stopped beside the hedge several metres away.

The entrance had two giant coffins standing upright on either side. Inside the coffins, two robot Horrors stared straight ahead and waved goodbye.

"Look. In their foreheads," Matt said, pointing. "Cameras. Probably security cameras. If we go in the entrance, the Monster Police will see us."

"We can squeeze through the hedge," a girl named Abby said. "Quick – no one is looking."

I lowered my shoulder and shoved my way

through the thick, prickly hedge. Everyone followed. A few seconds later, we all burst out, brushing needles from our clothes and hair.

We stopped in the shadow of the hedge to look around. Goodbye Land was an enormous park. Trees and grass and flower beds. Very peaceful looking. Like a graveyard.

"I don't see an exit," I said. "But what's that ride over there?"

This part of the park was nearly deserted. We trotted over to the ride. It stood under a round red canopy. It was called the R.I.P.P.E.R. DIPPER.

I saw a sign beside the entrance: WARNING! THIS RIDE GOES ONLY ONE WAY – DOWN!

"Let's ride it," Sheena said.

"But how can it help us?" I asked.

"It might take us to the underground tunnels," Matt replied. "We were already down there, but they chased us out," he explained to me. "If we can get back to the tunnels, we can follow them out of HorrorLand."

The alarm sirens were still rising and falling on the other side of the hedge.

"I just want to know one thing," I told Matt. "Why are you all so anxious to get out of here?"

"No time to explain," Matt said. "Trust us. We're in real danger. Stick with us, Boone. You really have no choice."

No more talk. I followed him into the short, dark entryway. A line of small, square black cars stood in front of us. The cars were on a track. The track led straight to a wide hole in the ground. Room for only one person in a car.

We all scrambled into cars. I lowered myself into the nearest one and pulled a safety bar over me. I grabbed the steering wheel with both hands and spun it.

The steering wheel was a fake. It didn't control the car.

A few seconds later, the ride started up. My hands flew off the wheel. My whole body jerked back hard as a deafening roar rose up all around me. And then I flew up off the seat as the car began to plunge – straight down!

I gripped the safety bar with all my might as the car dropped, picking up speed as it fell. The tyres whistled on the tracks. The air grew hot.

Faster. . .

Into total darkness. The ride was completely black, except for tiny yellow sparks that flew off the wheels of the car above me.

I hate fast rides, especially when you can't see where you're going.

Squeezed into this tiny car dropping into the pitch black, I thought: *This is a lot like being buried – only at a hundred miles an hour!*

"Oww!" I let out a startled cry as my car bumped the one beneath it.

I felt a hard jolt. My car rocked – and started to spin.

I shut my eyes.

And then the car stopped with a shattering jolt. Was the ride broken? How were we going to get out of here?

"What's going on?" a voice yelled.

"Help!"

Suddenly, the safety bar slid out of my hands.

"Huh?" I cried. Before I could catch my breath, the bottom of the car flew open with a loud *SNAP*!

And I toppled out into black space.

"AAAAAIIIII!" A hoarse scream burst from my throat as I fell.

I flew through the darkness, screaming all the way down.

Gazing up, I saw Matt plummeting towards me. And other kids falling. Everyone falling.

A hot wind rushed past me as I dropped through the blackness.

I shut my eyes. And pictured my family. Mom . . . Dad . . . Heather. . .

The last faces I would ever see.

"Unnnnh." The breath shot out of me as I landed. Landed hard on my back.

I bounced. Once. Twice.

Struggled to breathe.

THUD. THUD.

Kids crashed down all around me. Their hard falls sent me bouncing some more.

"Are we *alive*?" someone asked.

I struggled to regain my breathing. My heart pounded like crazy.

I sat up and squinted into glaring grey light. "Hey – it's some kind of mattress!" I managed to cry.

We had all landed on an enormous air mattress.

"It's a free-fall ride," Carly Beth said. "I guess we were *supposed* to fall."

Some kids laughed. A few kids cheered. We were all happy to be alive.

But it didn't take long to remember the trouble we were in.

"Can we get to the tunnels from here?" Matt wondered. "Hurry. Climb off this thing. Let's go."

Before I could slide to the floor, I felt a hard grip on my shoulder.

I spun around – and stared into the scowling face of a gigantic green-and-purple Horror.

A bunch of big, powerful-looking Horrors surrounded the air mattress. And Ned stepped forward. He wasn't smiling.

"Well, you survived the R.I.P.P.E.R. DIPPER," he said. "Good work, everyone."

He motioned for the Horrors to grab us. "Now let's see what thrills and chills The Keeper has in store for you. . ."

No way we could escape. The Horrors forced us to a rickety lift that took us back up to the surface. Then they marched us through the park.

Some park visitors cheered us as we passed by. They probably thought it was a parade or something.

The Horrors walked us across Zombie Plaza. I saw shops, and food carts, and game booths. Other kids were having fun. Why couldn't we?

We came to the Haunted Theatre. Above the

entrance, the marquee read: MONDO THE MAGICAL.

Were they taking us into a magic show?

No. The Horrors guided us into a little shop at the side of the theatre. The shop was called MONDO'S TRICKS AND TREATS.

I guessed Mondo was selling his magic tricks there. The shelves were filled. I passed a display of boxes that read: A MONDO EXCLUSIVE! PULL A HAT OUT OF A RABBIT!

No time to look at the store. The Horrors pushed us behind a curtain towards a little room at the back. At the far wall, a steep staircase led straight down.

Our shoes clattered on the metal stairs. No one spoke.

The stairs led to another flight of stairs. And then another. I realized we were now three floors beneath the park.

My throat suddenly felt dry. Despite the hot air down there, my hands were cold.

This was way scary. What did they plan to do with us? Just lock us up and keep us down there?

We stepped out into bright lights. A huge room with furry orange and green chairs and sofas. Sunlight-yellow wallpaper with blue fish all over it. A big zebra-skin rug. A purple-and-white polka-dot table with big claws on the legs. A floor lamp with red and white stripes like a barber pole.

So many colours, it was almost *blinding* down there! And all the furniture was totally weird looking and crazy.

"Where are we?" I demanded. "Where have you taken us?"

"You will be safe here," Ned said. "Unless you get on the wrong side of The Keeper. Be careful with him. Do everything he tells you. He is called The Keeper, but there is one thing he *can't* keep. He can't *keep* his cool!"

"You can't do this!" Matt screamed. "Let us out – now!"

"See you soon," Ned said. The door slammed shut behind him.

A hush fell over the room. We stood blinking, gazing around at the crazy colours and weird furniture.

Finally, a boy named Robby Schwartz broke the silence. "There's no one else down here. Let's break out," he said.

"How?" Abby demanded. "We're a *kilometre* beneath the park!"

"I didn't hear Ned lock the door," I said. I ran to it. Tried it. Wrong. It was locked.

"Look. Another room," Matt said. He pointed to a curtained doorway on the far wall.

We burst into the next room. It was just as big as the first, with bright colours everywhere. The room was cluttered with strange junk. Some kind of storeroom, probably.

I saw a rusted suit of armour leaning in one corner. A stuffed raven with a stuffed mouse in its mouth. A huge fish skeleton in a glass case.

Suddenly, Abby let out a scream. "No – I don't *believe* it!" she groaned.

She stared at a mummy propped up in a chair. The wrappings were yellowed and stained. The mummy's head tilted to one side.

But Abby was staring in horror at its middle. The ancient wrappings over the mummy's stomach had been *ripped open*!

Before I could ask why she was so upset, I heard a scream behind me. Carly Beth pointed to something on a low table. A rubber mask. "Sabrina," she cried. "The Haunted Mask! How . . . how did it follow me here?"

"There's something very wrong here," Julie said in a trembling voice. She pointed to an old camera inside a glass case. "Th-that camera is *evil*! It gave me so much trouble back home!"

Billy and Sheena were wide-eyed, frozen in front of an oil painting of a one-legged pirate. "Captain Jack!" Sheena murmured, shaking her head.

Carly Beth turned away from the ugly mask. "Don't you see what's happening?" she said. "All the hideous things that happened to us back home . . . they've all followed us to HorrorLand!"

"But – how?" Robby asked. "Do you think someone *knew* we all had horrifying adventures back home? Do you think that's why we were

125

invited here?"

Before anyone could answer, a door slammed behind us. A strangely costumed figure bounced into the room.

And Robby went pale. His mouth fell open, and he screamed, "No! No way! It's *impossible*! It *can't* be!"

10

Robby staggered back until he hit the wall.

The man wore a long, flowing leopard-skin cape over a bright orange superhero costume. His yellow-feathered boots came up to his knees. His hair was covered by an orange hood. His eyes were dark and round and rolled crazily in his head.

"I AM THE KEEPER!" he boomed in a deep, thundering voice.

Robby took a step forward. "No, you're NOT!" he cried. "You're Dr Maniac!"

The man brushed back his cape. "Wowie wow wow. Guess I'm more famous than I thought!"

"You're not famous!" Robby screamed. "I *created* you!"

The weird superhero tossed back his head and laughed at the ceiling. He had a high-pitched giggle of a laugh. He giggled for a long time, holding his sides.

Then he turned back to Robby, and his expression turned angry. "Kid, why don't you turn your teeth around and bite your face! You've got it all backward, dummo. I created YOU!"

"LIAR!" Robby screamed. He wasn't frightened now. He seemed way angry. "You're a liar!"

"I'm not a liar!" the superhero boomed. "I'm a MANIAC!"

Again, he tossed back his head and giggled up at the ceiling.

I turned to Robby, who was now red-faced and trembling. "What's with this guy?" I asked.

Robby pulled a drawing out of his backpack. "Look. Look at this. I drew him in a comic strip." Robby held it up so everyone could see. "I don't understand how he can be standing here. I . . . I *made him up*!"

Dr Maniac swiped the drawing from Robby's hand. He examined it for two seconds. "It looks a *little* like me," he said. "Not quite right around the chin. I'm much better looking than that!"

He ripped the drawing into shreds – and stuffed the shreds into his mouth.

"This guy is crazy," I whispered to Robby.

"I'm not crazy – I'm a MANIAC!" the superhero screamed again. He spat out shreds of the paper.

"And I'm The Keeper. Don't any of you think about escape. You can't escape from a MANIAC! HAHAHAHAHA!"

"Why were we invited to this park?" Matt demanded. "Why are you keeping us here now?"

"That's for me to know and for you to find out!" Dr Maniac bellowed.

"You can't keep us prisoner down here," Matt said.

"But that's my job!" the superhero cried. He giggled again. "Keeping you here is EASY! That's why they call me The Keeper! They don't call me The Let-'Em-Goer – do they?"

Matt clenched his hands into fists. "We have you outnumbered," he said.

"Ooh, I'm scared. I'm SCARED!" the superhero moaned. He made his whole body shake as if he were frightened.

Then he stepped up to the wall and threw a switch. "Why don't you all take a walk?" he cried.

"Whoa!" I uttered a startled gasp as the floor started to move beneath us.

I saw Carly Beth and Robby stumble and fall on to their backs.

I started walking, struggling to keep my balance.

The floor was rolling underneath us, moving faster and faster.

"Stop it! Stop it!" we screamed.

But Dr Maniac tilted his head back and drowned out our cries with his insane laughter.

11

The floor of the room was a giant treadmill. We had to walk faster... faster... to keep up with it.

Dr Maniac raised himself off the floor and floated in front of us. "Keep in step, people!" he ordered. "A few hours of walking will show you that The Keeper means business."

He giggled. "Don't thank me. Just throw money! HAHAHAHA. I've got plenty more activities planned. Anyone like to play Hangman? We'll play it later – with a *real noose*!"

I was jogging pretty hard to keep my balance. My heart was pounding, and my chest began to ache.

Robby was trotting next to me. He was having a tough time. I could see he was thinking hard, unable to believe what was happening. I guess he was kind of in shock.

Suddenly, the door burst open – and *another*

superhero darted into the room. This dude was huge, with enormous biceps and a massive chest.

His top and tights were bright purple. They matched his cape and his boots. He was a totally purple guy, except for his face, which was tomato-red.

"No!" Robby cried out. "No. It *can't* be! The Purple Rage!"

"Did you make *him* up, too?" I asked, huffing and puffing as I kept my legs going.

Robby nodded.

The Purple Rage flew up beside Dr Maniac. "Do you know what CRUNCHES my POTATO CRISPS?" he cried.

"This is *good* news," Robby muttered to me. "They are mortal enemies. They hate each other's guts. The Rage will *rescue* us!"

"Are you sure?" I murmured. I pointed.

The two superheroes were *hugging*.

"Know what FLIPS my ROOSTER?" the Purple Rage boomed. "Working together with you! I've always wanted to work with a MANIAC!"

He turned to us. "Keep walking," the Rage said. "Walk till you SQUAWK!"

"Now I get it!" Robby cried breathlessly. "Everyone – do you get it? Listen to me! If Dr Maniac and the Purple Rage are working together – that must mean that *all* the bad guys we defeated back home are working together!"

Some kids gasped.

"I get it," Carly Beth said. "They're working together – against *us*!"

I didn't understand what Robby and Carly Beth meant. I only knew that my legs were aching, and I was out of breath from walking so fast to stay on my feet.

I turned to the Purple Rage. Breathlessly, I called out, "You mean you're not going to rescue us from that *maniac*?"

The Rage let out a deep growl. His face turned as purple as his costume. I could swear I saw *steam* pour out of his ears.

He rushed forward and grabbed the front of my shirt. "You've really BURNED my BUTTER DISH!" he shouted in my face. "I'm going to make an *example* of you, punk! Watch this, everyone! Watch what the Mighty Rage does to this smart guy!"

"No! Let *me* do it!" Dr Maniac pushed the Purple Rage out of the way. "Here's a hot new trick I learned."

He began rubbing the palms of his gloved hands together, faster and faster. "Watch carefully. I can set my hands on fire. A little trick taught to me by the Scorch."

He rubbed his gloves harder. Faster. Smoke

132

rose up between them.

He turned to the Rage. "Do you know the Scorch? Nice guy. But he's got a fiery temper! HAHAHAHA!"

The Rage shoved Dr Maniac aside. "Know what WILTS my WALLABY? Waiting for you to take care of this punk! You're taking too long!"

He wrapped his purple gloves around my throat and lifted me up by the neck. Then he turned to the other kids. "I used to earn a little extra money by making balloon animals," he said. "What animal should I twist this guy into? Come on – don't everyone speak at once!"

Was this a joke? Some kind of comic-book superhero joke?

I shut my eyes and prayed it was a joke.

But I knew it was real. I knew we were all totally helpless against these insane nuts. Helpless – and doomed.

I tried to cry out as the Purple Rage began to twist my arms behind me. But he was squeezing my neck so tightly, I couldn't speak. I couldn't breathe.

"How about a nice poodle?" he said. "Or should I twist you into a giraffe with a long, long neck?"

To be continued in . . .

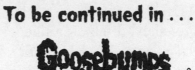

⑩ HELP! WE HAVE STRANGE POWERS!

DEAD, BATS & BEYOND:
SUPERVILLAIN OUTFITTERS

SHACKLES	
5 @ $39.99	$199.95
BEAR TRAP	
1 @ $49.99	$49.99
TRIP WIRE	
2 @ $12.99	$25.98
SOUND-PROOFING KIT	
1 @ $129.99	$129.99
YELLOW FEATHERS	
1 @ $9.99	$9.99
NETS	
3 @ $24.99	$74.97
WHITE SHOE POLISH (SALE)	
4 @ $4.99	$19.96
TOTAL:	$510.83

TO-DO LIST

1. PICK UP TIGHTS FROM DRY CLEANERS
2. MEND RIP IN LEOPARD-SKIN CAPE
3. FINISH TRAPDOOR INSTALLATION
4. PAY LATE FEE FOR DvD RENTALS
5. SEND FLOWERS AND CARD TO S.S.
6. DEFROST MEATBALLS

STAGGER INN

Dear Stagger Inn Patron,

As someone who has shown superior fright skills, you are eligible for our VIV (Very Important Villain) Treatment. Here is a sample of the items available to make your stay at the Stagger Inn as horrific as possible. You'll find more luxury scares in the Welcome Packet in your room.

PERSONAL CARE
- ❑ Dress Capes
- ❑ Soiled Rags
- ❑ Vat of Slime
- ❑ Wood Polish

FIND THE REST at
WWW.ESCAPEHorrorLAND.COM
—LIZZY

SMALL SNACKS
- ❑ Organs & Entrails
- ❑ Scorpion Feed (we need 24 hours' notice to collect guests)
- ❑ Squirrel (rotten, roasted, or still wriggling)
- ❑ Vat of Slime

Please contact Stagger Inn Desk Services if you would like any of these items to be waiting in your room when you arrive.

Before HorrorLand,
another camp gone wrong
starred in

THE HORROR AT CAMP JELLYJAM

Take a peek
at R.L. Stine's bone-chilling classic.
Now available with exclusive
new bonus features –
including the top five scariest campfire stories!

"I win!" Elliot cried. He jumped up and raised both fists in triumph.

"Three out of five!" I demanded, rubbing my wrist. "Come on – three out of five. Unless you're chicken."

I knew that would get him. Elliot can't stand to be called a chicken. He settled back in the seat.

We leaned over the narrow table and clasped hands. We had been arm wrestling for about ten minutes. It was kind of fun because the table bounced every time the trailer rolled over a bump in the road.

I am as strong as Elliot. But he's more determined. A *lot* more determined. You never saw anyone groan and sweat and strain so much in arm wrestling!

To me, a game is just a game. But to Elliot, every game is life-or-death.

He had won two out of three about five times. My wrist was sore, and my hand ached. But I really wanted to beat him in this final match.

I leaned over the table and squeezed his hand harder. I gritted my teeth and stared menacingly into his dark brown eyes.

"Go!" he cried.

We both strained against each other. I pushed hard. Elliot's hand started to bend back.

I pushed harder. I nearly had him. Just a little harder.

He let out a groan and pushed back. He shut his eyes. His face turned beet-red. I could see the veins push out at the sides of his neck.

My brother just can't stand to lose.

SLAM!

The back of my hand hit the table hard.

Elliot had won again.

Actually, I let him win. I didn't want to see his whole head explode because of a stupid arm-wrestling match.

He jumped up and pumped his fists, cheering for himself.

"Hey!" he cried out as the trailer swayed hard, and he went crashing into the wall.

The trailer lurched again. I grabbed the table to keep from falling off my seat. "What's going on?"

"We changed direction. We're heading down now," Elliot replied. He edged his way back towards the table.

But we bumped hard, and he toppled to the floor. "Hey – we're going backwards!"

"I'll bet Mom's driving," I said, holding on to the table edge with both hands.

Mom always drives like a crazy person. When you warn her that she's going eighty, she always says, "That can't be right. It feels as if I'm going thirty-five!"

The trailer was bouncing and bumping, rolling downhill. Elliot and I were bouncing and bumping with the trailer.

"What is their problem?" Elliot cried, grabbing on to one of the beds, struggling to keep his balance. "Are they backing up? Why are we going backwards?"

The trailer roared downhill. I pushed myself up from the table and stumbled to the front to see the car. Shoving aside the red plaid curtain, I peered out through the small window.

"Uh . . . Elliot. . ." I choked out. "We've got a problem."

"Huh? A problem?" he replied, bouncing harder as the trailer picked up speed.

"Mom and Dad aren't pulling us any more," I told him. "The car is gone."

Elliot's face filled with confusion. He didn't understand me. Or maybe he didn't believe me!

"The trailer has come loose!" I screamed, staring out the bouncing window. "We're rolling downhill – on our own!"

"N-n-n-no!" Elliot chattered. He wasn't stuttering. He was bouncing so hard, he could barely speak. His trainers hopped so hard on the trailer floor, he seemed to be tap-dancing.

"OW!" I let out a pained shriek as my head bounced against the ceiling. Elliot and I stumbled to the back. Gripping the windowsill tightly, I struggled to see where we were heading.

The road curved steeply downhill, through thick pine woods on both sides. The trees were a bouncing blur of greens and browns as we hurtled past.

Picking up speed. Bouncing and tumbling.

Faster.

Faster.

The tyres roared beneath us. The trailer tilted and dipped.

I fell to the floor. Landed hard on my knees. Reached to pull myself up. But the trailer swayed, and I went sprawling on my back.

Pulling myself to my knees, I saw Elliot bouncing around on the floor like a football. I threw myself at the back of the trailer and peered out the window.

The trailer bumped hard. The road curved sharply – but we didn't curve with it!

We shot off the side of the road. Swerved into the trees.

"Elliot!" I shrieked. "We're going to crash!"